A Divided Forest

The life, times, and lineage of
Roy Daniel Bailey

by
Doris Chapin Bailey

Front and Back Cover Photography
by David Dapcevich SitkaPhotos

Order this book online at www.trafford.com/07-1493
or email orders@trafford.com

Most Trafford titles are also available at major online book retailers.

Front and Back Cover Photography
by David Dapcevich SitkaPhotos

Note for Librarians: A cataloguing record for this book is available from Library
and Archives Canada at www.collectionscanada.ca/amicus/index-e.html

Printed in Victoria, BC, Canada.

ISBN: 978-1-4251-3761-8

*We at Trafford believe that it is the responsibility of us all, as both individuals
and corporations, to make choices that are environmentally and socially sound.
You, in turn, are supporting this responsible conduct each time you purchase a
Trafford book, or make use of our publishing services. To find out how you are
helping, please visit www.trafford.com/responsiblepublishing.html*

*Our mission is to efficiently provide the world's finest, most comprehensive
book publishing service, enabling every author to experience success.
To find out how to publish your book, your way, and have it available
worldwide, visit us online at www.trafford.com/10510*

Trafford
PUBLISHING   www.trafford.com

North America & international
toll-free: 1 888 232 4444 (USA & Canada)
phone: 250 383 6864 ♦ fax: 250 383 6804 ♦ email: info@trafford.com

The United Kingdom & Europe
phone: +44 (0)1865 722 113 ♦ local rate: 0845 230 9601
facsimile: +44 (0)1865 722 868 ♦ email: info.uk@trafford.com

10 9 8 7 6 5 4 3

This book is dedicated
to our mentors in the Tlingit culture:

Lydia George
Jimmy George
Garfield George
Mark Jacobs, Jr.
Bertha Karras

Doris Chapin Bailey was born and grew up in southern Idaho where outdoor activity was an important part of her life. When she married Roy in 1973, they had discovered they had a great deal in common: a love of life and the outdoors; a fondness for the quiet and beauty of nature; and a need for a close companionship. Over the years, as she slowly learned the details of Roy's childhood, she felt a strong compulsion to put those stories to paper. This small book is the result of that compulsion. She hopes it adds to the history of the many Tlingits of her husband's generation who were taken from their culture and suffered the loss of belonging that was inevitable. There are many lessons to be learned, ideas to be cultivated, and a brighter future to be sought in this writing. Roy and Doris continue to live in Sitka, Alaska, where they enjoy the seasons of life, and the magnificent scenery and wildlife that is Southeast Alaska.

Author's Note:

This book would not have come to fruition without the help, advice, and encouragement of good friends. First is the encouragement I received from my husband, about whom this book is written. Although his innermost feelings would say "Don't do this," he seems to understand how important it is to me to save the unique story that is his.

I could not have begun or finished this endeavor without the assistance of friends. I was humbled and overwhelmed by those who helped me along the way. Thank you to Stacey Woolsey, who read the manuscript and made suggestions that made the whole idea of actually writing this and publishing it seem possible. Thank you to Gayle Hammons, who, with unfailing cheerfulness, took the text apart and showed me how to put it back together again, with more clarity and interest. Thank you to Roby Littlefield, who read it with an eye to the Tlingit orthography, and who made some gentle suggestions on deletions. And a big thanks to Rory Schneeberger with her unflagging enthusiasm and expertise who made some very insightful suggestions. With the editing help of these women, this book was completed.

The list of "thank you's" would not be complete without mentioning my daughter, Janice Walker, who helped with computer formatting and the pictures to be included. Her expertise was gratefully received. Thank you, Jan.

A huge thank you goes to the Sitka Historical Society and Director Robert Medinger who used the Society's equipment and his expertise in scanning and manipulating some of the images. This was of enormous help.

The cover photography, done by Dave Dapcevich, was suggested by my daughter Jan, and the protocol and logistics were arranged by Garfield George. It was one of the most thrilling moments in the entire process. It was a ceremony within a ceremony. I cannot say thank you sufficiently to those responsible for this "icing on the cake."

And, I cannot end without mentioning the assistance of Harold Jacobs and Jimmy George. Without their input, I could not have told the story of the U.S. Navy bombardment of Killisnoo. Via telephone, e-mail, and in person, they gave me assistance and encouragement. Also many thanks to Heather Lende who gave permission for me to re-print her *Anchorage Daily News* article, "'Gunalchéesh' — Tlingit for 'thank you' — says volumes."

Sue Thoreson of the Sitka National Historical Park, Steve Henrickson of the State of Alaska State Library Historical Collections, and Robert Preucel of the University of Pennsylvania each assisted greatly in securing use of historical photos for inclusion. Thank you!

Thanks go to Kristen Griffin, Robert Medinger, and Major Joe Murray of the Salvation Army who read the manuscript and offered thoughtful and thorough critique. And, without the gentle encouragement of those to whom this book is dedicated, I would not have been able to begin. Roy's *Deisheetaan* (Raven) sister and nephews have been so kind and thoughtful in their teaching. My own adopted *Dakl'aweidí* (Eagle) brother and sister have assisted with love to teach me things I needed to know. My hope is that I learned what they tried to teach.

Thank you one and all. *Gunulchéesh!*

INTRODUCTION

By way of acknowledgment to my wife and to the readers
of this book
From Roy Daniel Bailey - July, 2007

My name is *Saant.éex̱*
I am of the *Deisheetaan* Clan of Angoon
I belong to the End of the Trail House (*Deishú hít*)
My mother was *Took Tláa* of the *Deisheetaan*, *Deishú hít*
My father was *Waank'* of the *Chookaneidí* Clan of Sitka
My Uncle *Gaaxwéi* was the Clan Leader of Sitkoh Bay
(Chatham)
At Sitkoh Bay, there is a Cave there Called, *Yéil katóogu.*
Next to it is a stream where sockeyes run
And right next to the Cave is spring water
We use these as our main Emblem. Which we call

Yéil katóogu, tinaa gooní
Which basically means "Raven Cave with Copper Shields
in the spring water."
There is a story told by Klukwan People. That on a bright
day, the Copper
Shields in the spring water shine so brightly, they could
see it from Klukwan.
That is to say, "That they could feel the warmth and
Respect we have for
them and nature. And they are engulfed by this Warmth.
And I say to you, "Let this Warmth and Respect that
shines from my Uncle's
Land embrace you too, this day."
Yéi á!
Gunalchéesh!

TLINGIT PRONUNCIATION

(This is not a complete pronunciation chart for consonants)

Vowel Chart

a = like English *was*
aa = like the Swedish car *Saab*
e = like the number *ten*
ei = like the number *eight*
i = like English *hit*
ee = like the number *teen*
u = like English *put*
oo = like English *moon*

The letter *L* is voiceless, sounds like a lisp, and is not used in English. Put your tongue on the top of your mouth and blow out both sides of the tongue to come up with the *L* sound. Use the *L* sound described here for *tl* as in *Tlingit,* which is the English spelling of the word *Lingít.* The underlined *g*, *k* and *x* are pronounced in the back of the throat. Sometimes this is written with an *H* after the letter such as gh, kh or xh. These are also sounds not used in English. The apostrophe after a consonant is a "pinched" sound; hold your breath for a split second while your tongue makes the sound. A period in the middle of a word means it sounds like two words. In English, this could look like *co.op or uh.oh.*

A tone mark over a vowel means your voice rises (in pitch, not volume).

An English example is *Mérry/Marée.* Everything else is just like English.

Table of Contents

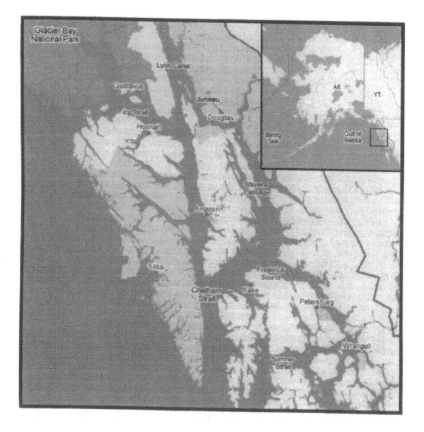

FORWARD

This is a story that is crying to be told. I have resisted writing it far too long. Now I must put words down to keep the story from being lost. It is a story that has been repeated in many different forms for the past one hundred years – each story is unique and many have been lost forever.

I am Doris Chapin Bailey, wife of Roy Bailey, and I apologize in advance for any errors I may make when I talk about the rich and varied Tlingit heritage. I have only respect and admiration for this great people. My Tlingit name is *Sxaalgén*. I was adopted in Klukwan, Alaska, by Mark Jacobs, Jr., (*Gusht'eiheen*) of the *Dakl'aweidí*, during the Alaska Native Brotherhood Grand Camp Convention in 1989. He gave me his mother's name, which was a huge honor. I am humbled by this tribute.

All the words set upon these pages are mine alone. There is no intent to violate protocol or denigrate any person, clan, or story. The primary reason for this narrative is to set down the story as remembered by Roy, or as remembered by me as told by Roy.

Descriptions of cultural connotations are not intended to be substantive. They are an attempt to describe how the changing culture wreaked havoc in individual lives. In other words, this is not intended as a scholarly work, but as the story of a person who was born in the early part of the 20th century, a story showing how the clan and the family and individuals were shaped by the hurricane of a changed and changing culture. Any conclusions I state are mine alone and are not intended to be taken in any absolute terms.

Many statements of Roy's are so descriptive of who Roy is and how his thinking processes work, that they take my breath away. I have tried to transcribe those statements as closely to his actual words as possible so the reader will feel the depth of his selflessness and his love of nature. Whenever an emphasis is added to a statement, that emphasis is mine.

There are times that I record stories that I heard many years ago that I did not understand well at that time. I was not knowledgeable enough then to even know the questions I should have asked. So I have told the story, but any concrete conclusions are impossible to draw because no questions were asked.

Also it should be noted that in Alaska, the words

Native, Indian and *Tlingit* are used in everyday language as synonyms.

This work has taken me four years, but it has been a labor of love for this man who, despite all he has encountered on his life's journey, has always been true to himself. So I say to my dear husband, "What a monumental accomplishment!"

CHAPTER ONE

Beginnings

In a world of soaring eagles and mischievous ravens, tall, green, snow-capped mountains coming straight down to the sea, with mists and rain seemingly endless, love stories were bound to occur. An Aleut man who was raised as a Tlingit, whose name was *Waank'* (Charlie Bailey Sr.) and a Tlingit girl, whose name was *Took Tláa* (Sophie Paul) are believed to have fallen in love and married in about 1922. Their first child, *Shakwaanee Éesh*, Charlie Jr., was born in 1923. We think his birthplace was Sitka. Their second child, Roy Daniel Bailey, *Kaaxoo.átch*, was born on November 5, 1926, in Petersburg, Alaska. Roy was called *Kaaxoo.átch* by his mother. The name *Saant.éex* was bestowed upon him as an honor by Lydia George at a *koo.éex'* held in Angoon by the *Deisheetaan* in 2000. He follows his mother's Raven lineage *Deisheetaan, Deishú hít* which is called "End of the Trail House."

Charlie Sr. and Sophie both spoke Tlingit as their first language as did Charlie Jr. Charlie Sr. was born in 1901, and Sophie was born in 1907, as far as we know. It is believed their marriage was a love match. Perhaps they were not married in the white man's way, or perhaps they were married in the Russian Orthodox Church. Since all the Sitka Russian Church records were burned in the fire of 1966, and no one thought to ask Charlie Sr. all these questions before his death in 1978, no one will ever know. All those who might have had answers are now gone. By doing the simple math, it can be determined that Sophie was 16 when Charlie Jr. was born. She came of age during the late teens and early 20's of the 20th century. This is a time when so much of the Tlingit culture was lost forever.

Charlie and Sophie were not from Petersburg, so why Roy was born there is not known. They may have been there fishing or working for a cannery, both of which we know they did in later years. Roy was born in November, so it was past time for summer fish camp. It would have probably been cold and rainy, which is a normal weather pattern for that time of year. Sophie may have been helped by local or visiting Native women, or she may have given birth alone, or with Charlie, although it seems unlikely by the white man's standards of that day that Charlie was present. The birth was not recorded in any white man's recording method. We are not aware of what traditional help may have been available.

After the birth of Roy came two sisters: Carmen in 1927 or 1928, and May in 1930.

There are some memories of this early time and it is interesting to look at the things Roy remembers. These memories are not all of bad times – although those stories seem to prevail. Roy remembers someone calling him "_Kaaxoo.átch_" when he was very small – like a mother calling her son home for dinner. We like to think that is what he is remembering. Walter Soboleff, a much-esteemed Tlingit elder and Presbyterian minister, has told Roy about Mrs. L. C. Berg putting Roy in a fish box for a nap when Walter and Roy's father worked together at the Cold Storage in Sitka. Did these things happen before or after his mother died? Was his mother ill at the time? Had she already died?

Hunger! The children were hungry. That is definitely remembered – there was no food in the house. The boys, Roy and Charlie, found a silver can with a wire handle on it labeled "Karo." They knew better than to eat what was in the can without asking, as they were told it was for Baby May. There were also two crusts of bread which they were not allowed to eat either. Imagine the little boy that Roy was, "sitting by the window, watching the seagulls, feeling so sad **for the family** because we didn't have any food." He went on to say, "I watched the sea gulls flying by or some that just seemed to float in one spot without moving their wings. I know what hunger is for a small child." This memory seems especially significant to me since Roy could not have been more than 3 or 4 at the time.

Roy's sister Carmen probably from 1950's Picture courtesy of Paul and Ethel Willis.

Roy's brother Charlie Jr. hunting in Deep Inlet. Probably 1940's. Picture courtesy of Gene Riggs.

Roy's sister Mary (May) and her husband Bobby Duncan in 1978 in Sitka

Roy's father and stepmother Charlie Sr. and Olinda with Roy in the Pioneer Home in Sitka in 1978

Two stories have come to light that Roy remembers from his early years before his mother died. Both incidents could have been fatal and add to the credibility of Charlie Sr.'s statement to Roy: "It's a wonder you lived to grow up!"

Playing on the float at Bredvik's Grocery Store (where Bailey's used to stand on Katlian Street, now a parking lot where the Women in Fisheries Marine Memorial brick wall is located), Roy remembers falling off into the water. The thing that sticks in his mind the most was seeing and feeling the barnacles as he went down through the water. The next thing he remembers is looking up and being on his back on the float with lots of people looking down at him – a small remnant in his memory that remains from that time. His brother Charlie was the one who pulled him out of the water.

The second small memory is of running across Katlian Street, being hit by a Model T Ford, and looking up at the bottom of the car as it was going over him. The car stopped and his father pulled him out from under the chassis. There were not many cars in Sitka at that time, and Roy was quite interested in this strange machine. Fortunately, Model T's sat high off the road!

Roy also remembers being tied in the bow of his father's round-bottomed double-ended boat in order to keep him "put" while his father fished. Roy accompanied his father as he rowed out to Biorka Island in this manner, probably in the late 20's. We are not sure if this was before or after his mother died.

When I met Roy's dad, Charlie Sr. in 1974, he was instantly recognizable as a sweet and kind man. If kindness is genetic, it's easy to realize where Roy's kindness comes from.

He would call me "Honey" and pat my hand. From what I've been told, he was an extremely strong man physically who worked very hard. Given this period in history, it seems reasonable to believe that Charlie, Sr. was unable to get one of the well-paying and steady jobs available in Sitka due to his being Aleut. This kind of occurrence was seldom discussed either in the day-to-day life of those times or now. We have received reports that Roy's dad worked for Louis Minard's family, chopping wood. He also chopped and stacked wood for the ANB (Alaska Native Brotherhood) Hall. We have Walter Soboleff's statement that Charlie worked at the Sitka Cold Storage. He worked for George Howard Sr. on the seiner *F/V Progress*, out of Todd Cannery. He fished both for the cannery which had employed fishermen – the cannery owned the boats – and as a self-employed commercial fisherman. Charlie Jr. and Roy bought Charlie Sr. a fishing boat sometime in the early 1940's. It was the end of the Depression and it was a hard life. On one occasion, Roy called his father "a hard luck fisherman" when he recalled the fishing boat he and his brother had purchased sinking in Kalinin Bay. There are accounts of Charlie Bailey hunting with Charlie Benson in the book *Haa Aaní, Our Land*.

Charlie Sr. in Kalinin Bay circa 1938

Roy remembers Charlie Benson as a special friend of his father's. On different occasions, he also had as fishing partners Lawrence Widmark Sr. and John Abbott, Sr. When he was a boy, Charlie Sr. was part of a small crew that went hunting for fur seals in a row boat – "so far out that Mt. Edgecumbe appeared as a sea gull on the horizon," according to Charlie in 1975. It is hard to imagine rowing a boat so far out on the open ocean and then staying there, waiting and looking for a fur seal. (The so-called "gas boats" did not make their appearance until the 20's, and then they were expensive to buy and maintain.) We neither know how often these fur seal hunting trips happened, nor how the seals were dispatched for their pelts. Charlie did tell us that the remuneration he received was about 10 cents per pelt. (In the taking of seals, nothing on the seal was wasted – every part was used in some way, and still is today.)

While seal hunting, although it is possible hand-thrown spears were used, Roy speculates that the 30-30 Winchester was used at this point in time. This was not the sleek model of today, but would have had a large, long, octagon-shaped barrel. Weapons of this type would not have been plentiful, as they were financially out of reach for most people. We place this memory between 1910 and maybe (although not likely) into the 20's.

It is unknown when Sophie became ill with tuberculosis, or even if it was tuberculosis. Oral tradition says it was tuberculosis. In 1930, Charlie took Sophie home to Angoon, to either get treatment or to die. Roy was left with the Jones family in Sitka when Charlie Sr. took Sophie home to Angoon. Lydia George (in the clan custom, Lydia would be Roy's sister) tells us that both Charlie Jr. and Carmen were in Angoon when Sophie was ill, but she does not remember whether they were there when she died, so they may have been with other families. Lydia would have been about 8 years old. Roy learned of his mother's death when one of the Jones' boys asked him why he wasn't crying.

When Charlie Sr. returned to Sitka, he came back with Charlie Jr. and Carmen only. Baby May was left in Angoon to become the daughter of Elizabeth Paul Brown Williams, the oldest of Sophie's sisters. Mrs. Williams was already up in age at the time she took in May. (Bobby Duncan always referred to Mrs. Williams as "the old lady.") Elizabeth changed May's name to Mary. There is some confusion as to May/Mary's birth date, either May 19th or 31st. (We've been told Mary chose May 19th as her birthday; this was also the birthday of one of her sons who died.)

Charlie Sr. married Olinda Search, a *Kiks.ádi* widow from Hoonah in about 1934. She was in need of a husband and Charlie Sr. hoped to have a home for his children. We've been told that Charlie Jr., because he was old enough to do chores, went from home to home to live. After Charlie Sr. and Olinda's marriage, Charlie Jr. lived with them off and on. Carmen was not old enough to do chores, but was too old to be desirable to adopt into a family so she, too, went from one family's home to another. Carmen apparently, from information given us by Lydia George, spent a lot of time in Angoon after she was old enough to be useful. It would appear that Roy was kept by his father as long as possible – a cherished son, but keeping him was a real problem for Charlie Sr. It was difficult to try to work to earn enough money to take care of the family. This was late 1930 or early 1931.

Charlie Sr. once told me about trying to find work and having someone tell him to sign some papers. He didn't know what he was signing, and only learned after it was too late that he had joined the Merchant Marines. Apparently this caused him to be gone from home for quite a while, and he was very unhappy about that.

I have often wondered if this incident may have been the reason Charlie Sr. took Roy to the orphanage in Juneau. This makes a great deal of sense to me as Charlie tried very hard to keep Roy with him before he reached school-age. As Roy puts it, "When I went into the orphanage, the family was truly split up. All contact with my brother and sisters was lost – all contact with my father was lost. No voice was heard from the family and this lonely existence continued on through the years of [our] growing up. All four children were left to find [our] way through life or fight for what [we] got – each was now in a family not of [our] choosing."

CHAPTER TWO

Cultural Discussion

I n 1904, Sitka's "last potlatch" was held, as the white man had, in his infinite wisdom, outlawed the ceremony which was and is a prominent load-bearing wall of the culture.

Perhaps a word about the English word *potlatch* and what it means is in order. Essentially, to the white man's way of thinking, a potlatch is a huge party. In fact, the word *party* is frequently used by Natives today, but the Tlingit word for the event is *koo.éex'* meaning "to be invited." Guests are fed at least two meals and all guests are given many gifts, with the most valuable being blankets. The hosts and those attending donate large amounts of money which is then given to special honorees and other guests in attendance. The hosts gain or lose status, relative to the value of the gifts and the amount of money given and distributed. These parties sometimes last several days and even in the current age, they will frequently last twenty-four hours or more. It is imperative for the hosts to belong to one clan or house, and the guests to belong to the opposite clan. One attends a _koo.éex'_ only by invitation.

Today, the most common party given is a memorial for one person (or sometimes more than one) who has died; the memorial takes place a year or more after the death. There is a fairly significant protocol to be followed, although this varies from community to community and even from clan to clan. These parties are held primarily in the fall of the year after the salmon have run and been preserved for the winter. Gifts of food may include salmon, halibut, berries, seal oil, herring eggs, venison, and other highly-prized local edibles. The Tlingit prefer the word _koo.éex'_ rather than _potlatch_, which is a white man's word with some very different connotations. The _koo. éex'_ is the time for the public showing of _at.óow. At.óow_ can be ceremonial regalia such as blankets, headdresses, bentwood boxes, paddles, daggers, and other artifacts which have been handed down from uncle to nephew for many generations. There might be several tables full of these revered items which are seldom seen but brought out on rare ceremonial occasions to show support, respect, honor, and status. The _koo.éex'_ is a time for the sharing of stories and songs, which are clan communal property. It is a time to mourn a passing, and to celebrate the life of someone who has passed; to pay debts of honor; to bring extended family together, and to bring back ancestral names by putting them on children and adoptees.

Traditionally, regalia is displayed and used during a _koo.éex'_. In the late 19th century and early 20th century, many Tlingit men put their treasured regalia away or even sold it. Some, rather than disgrace the family by selling an ancestor's artifact, held a traditional funeral service by burning or cremating such items. The men took to "wearing the three piece suit," as Jimmy George so succinctly called it. There are few photos of that time showing Tlingit men in their regalia that were not posed by a photographer. In speaking of this phenomenon, Jimmy and Garfield George spoke with some bitterness: "We have no proof of the clan possessions or regalia – our uncles are always shown in pictures in the three piece suit!!" The fathers put the regalia on their own children (as opposed to their nephews and nieces) for pictures and thus the regalia was lost in some cases to the opposite clan.

The following article by Heather Lende was published in the _Anchorage Daily News_ and, in my opinion, has so captured the joy and sorrow and need for balance that the Tlingit culture has, that I requested permission from her to include it here. She has kindly given me permission and I am hopeful it will give you, the reader, some insights into the _koo.éex'_.

'Gunalchéesh'—Tlingit for 'thank you'— says volumes

By HEATHER LENDE

Published: September 13, 2007

HAINES — By the time I was handed the thermal blanket, I was out of room on the table, my lap and the floor for any more gifts. I already had a bag of fruit and cans of Vienna sausages, pork and beans, fruit cocktail and corn. There were also socks, jars of jam, soap, coffee, microwave popcorn, pens, oven mitts, smoked salmon and lots of Top Ramen.

"It wouldn't be a potlatch without Top Ramen," my friend Tony said as we rose, waving a few packages in the air to Tlingit chanting.

I was glad for the activity. I was sleepy and very full. It was after midnight, more than 12 hours since the party began. I had eaten pilot bread, salmon spread, berries, moose stew, salmon and rice, prime rib with potatoes, gravy and carrots and, most recently, lox and cream cheese on a bagel. A Tlingit friend told me the only rule at a potlatch is never, ever say "No, thank you."

Like the other guests, I had left my seat only during the handful of designated five-minute breaks. In the daylight, I'd used them to walk around the village. But after dark, when the bears were out, I stayed closer to the back porch of the Klukwan Alaska

Native Sisterhood Hall.

The memorial party for a Tlingit leader from Juneau with Klukwan connections was like Thanksgiving, Christmas and Easter all in one, with food, gifts and the promise of heaven.

I was at the party because my husband was being adopted by his hunting partner, who was also the host. This tradition of inviting non-Natives into the family at these parties is an old one that honors connections in the community, confirms friendships and helps perpetuate the culture. It is generous and practical: Whenever they lose someone, they add a few more.

My husband will be an Eagle. In Tlingit culture, there are two equal and reciprocal halves, Ravens and Eagles, called moieties. They take care of each other. Every Tlingit is a Raven or an Eagle, and you marry into the opposite moiety. When an Eagle dies, the Ravens support them.

So now the Eagles were paying back the Ravens, and thanking them, with what is usually called a potlatch, or payoff party, but the proper term is _Koo.éex'_, which means to call or invite. The party also ends the mourning period.

This one was a continuation of a party that began in Juneau. The person it memorialized, Austin Brown, had lived there but had deep tribal roots here.

Since this was the happy half of the memorial (all the sad parts had been done), the Eagle hosts, who weren't allowed to sit at the tables but cooked, served, gave gifts and entertained us, had a lot of fun making their Raven guests smile.

They told jokes, some in Tlingit, most in English, and sang jazz standards and Tlingit songs.

Florence Sheakley, a woman I had pegged as a stern keeper-of-tradition type — she has steel-gray hair and teaches Tlingit-language classes at the university in Juneau — proved me wrong when she and her family did a "Mrs. Don Ho" musical revue that included singing "Tiny Bubbles" in Tlingit with Hawaiian costumes and hula dancing.

There was so much more — some slapstick, some solemn, some I understood, much I didn't — and all the while, more gifts were given and more food was served. A novel could be written about what happened to a Chilkat blanket by master weaver Anna Brown Ehlers. After formally presenting it as a gift, she said she would cut it up. There was a long silence as the blanket was taken down and she carefully sliced it into small pieces that she gave to special people.

The beautiful, rare blanket, worth thousands of dollars, was apparently destroyed to repair a tear in the fabric of the tribe that happened so long ago most of the folks didn't know the details. Anna's father had, though, and it was his dying wish that she do this to make whatever was wrong right again.

It was a huge display of faith in tradition, and a

powerful statement about the cultural significance of a Chilkat blanket versus its value as an art object. But it was way more than that. It may sound crazy now that she cut up her beautiful blanket, but in witnessing it, I felt holier than during anything I've seen in church.

When we finally poured out of the hall into the pre-dawn darkness and walked toward trucks and cars to the rhythm of the wind in the cottonwoods and the hum of the river — the same backbeat that has mixed with the songs of Klukwan villagers for thousands of years — I wondered how I could properly thank them for a seat at their table and an invitation to their party.

A note seemed too small. Then I remembered what an elder had said hours earlier: "If you just say 'Thank you,' that is a great speech. Sometimes, 'thank you' is the greatest speech you can give."

Roy has mentioned to me that he can remember being told over and over to "speak English" by Tlingit elders. He says, "The urging of the fathers and grandfathers [to speak English] was more successful than anyone realized it would be. It was so successful that it is now taking a determined effort to teach the language and for the young people to learn to speak it." Language is the key to cultural identity. I am encouraged by the determination of many to teach and learn the Tlingit language.

When speaking with a family member, (a doctoral candidate in anthropology whose thesis deals with the Lakota tribe), she told me that many of the world's matrilineal societies have suffered great and/or irreparable harm from dominant patriarchal societies which are so antithetical to a matrilineal one. In very simplistic terms and my own rationalization, I have come up with my own definition of *matrilineal* as it relates to the Tlingit culture. A matrilineal society means that the males are the leaders, decision makers, and orators, but it is through the females that status is earned, and all possessions are inherited or passed on.

The Tlingit had no concept of land as "property." Land was used and "owned" by the clan, and this included areas which were for hunting and fishing, summer fish camps and winter villages. Ownership in the white man's way of thinking did not exist. Someone could receive permission to "live" or to "hunt and fish" in certain locations from the clan who "owned the use of" that property, but the land itself continued to "belong" to the clan. This concept caused and causes many conflicts because it collides with the white man's belief in "ownership of real property."

The need to "write things down," a piece of the white man's culture, is becoming a necessary adjunct to Tlingit culture in order to "remember how it used to work" and "keep from totally forgetting." In my opinion, the ability to recite the history and protocol, which was a highly-regarded skill carefully taught and rigorously guarded by the uncles, is not promoted in every clan. In most cases, this is not because of carelessness or lack of desire, but because of the many stresses of living in today's world. Those who realize what's happening are hastening to write the Tlingit history.

This short and much simplified excursion into culture is made only because the upheaval of the culture caused the upheaval of families and of whole communities. In discussing the reason for the name of this story, meant to denote culture clash in Roy's life, the following comments from Roy in an August 2004 e-mail to Arnold Walker are used. Roy was responding to a newspaper article about loss of culture, and summed up his thoughts on culture clash in his own life: "......many other people can agree that they in turn have experienced instances where their separation [from the culture] was as significant as any other. For instance, I was raised in an orphanage where the Native speech and culture was washed out of us most thoroughly. Our mouths were washed out with soap if we talked the Tlingit language. I learned the taste of soap a long, long time ago. Eventually, I was the same as any white kid but, I am Tlingit. The learning of the language and culture at this late date is mostly superfluous. In other words, the learning would be beneficial but my lifestyle is the same... lost forever in the land of the white man but still [I] am a Tlingit. The square peg, and so forth, a true misfit but just row with the flow. Much to complain about but what good would it do? Meanwhile, just smile and let it go at that. Enjoy the coffee and the day and that's it."

CHAPTER THREE

Lineage

oy and I met (May) Mary Duncan upon the death of Roy's father in 1978. Both Roy and Mary were emotional about getting acquainted and pleased to finally know one another. At that time, Mary Duncan told us that she learned when she was about fifteen years old, that her father was Charlie Bailey of Sitka and that she had a brother named Roy. Elizabeth Williams, a half-sister of Sophie's, had raised Mary in Angoon. Elizabeth's mother was *Sooxsaan* whereas Sophie's mother was *Koodeishgé*; they had the same father and both mothers were *Deisheetaan*, so far as we know. We have conjectured that Elizabeth's mother may have died young, and that *Koodeishgé* was mother to John Paul's (*Kootla.aa*) earlier children from *Sooxsaan*, or possibly Elizabeth was already grown. According to information received from Harold

Jacobs, Elizabeth had four older full brothers. Elizabeth's mother's Tlingit name of *Sooxsaan* was given to Mary by Elizabeth instead of Sophie's mother's name. Sophie's full sisters, both older than she, were Annie (Ebona) and Florence (James). Florence was Lydia George's mother. Lydia has said she was about eight years old when Sophie was brought home to Angoon to die.

The following is the information we have been given regarding Roy's lineage. This information is from Lydia George, Jimmy George, and Harold Jacobs: (I hope I have recorded it correctly. Any errors are mine alone.)

X'aleix'w from the Grouse Fort, who is the father of

X'eijaak from Hoonah, who is the father of

Kootla.aa (John Paul Sr.) who married *Sooxsaan* who is assumed to be *Deisheetaan* with their children being:

> *Kashaxaaw* (Billy Billy)
> *Kooneik*
> *Daakashaan*

> *Kaatlein* (John Paul Jr., father of Annie Jacobs - Annie's mother was *Dakl'aweidi*)

> *S'igidu.oo*

> (*Daagunaak*) Elizabeth Paul Brown Williams raised Mary Duncan

then *Kootla.aa* (John Paul Sr.) married *Koodeishgé* (Mary) (*Deisheetaan*) with their children being:

K'eeyaal'tin (Annie Paul Ebona, Andy Ebona's grandmother)

Ḵaat'aawu (James Paul)

G'il'a.aan (Frank Paul)

Saant.éex (Jim Paul)

X'eiska (Florence Paul James, mother of Lydia George)

Took Tláa (Sophie Paul Bailey) born in 1907, died 1930 or 1931

Koodeishgé's mother was *Kaachkuldeix'* whose mother was *Tleiḵ'wás'i.*

Took Tláa (Sophie Paul Bailey) married *Waank'* (Charlie Dick Bailey) probably in about 1922. Their children:

Charlie Bailey Jr. (*Shaḵwáanee Éesh*), born 1923, died 1945

Roy Daniel Bailey (*Ḵaaxoo.átch* and *Saant.éex*) born 1926

Carmen Bailey born 1928 - unknown whereabouts - last heard from late 1960's

May (Mary) Bailey (Williams) Duncan (*Soox saan*) born 1930, died 2004

Carmen Bailey married David Howard Jr. and had 4 children:

John Howard born June 8, 1950, died March 18, 2002

Della Howard (Downs) born 1953 lives in Maryland

David Howard III born February 17, 1955, died August 25, 1990

Anita Marie Howard born July 20, 1957 (adopted in the white man's way by Roy and Doris Bailey in 1978).

David Howard Jr. also had another daughter, Genevieve Guanzon, who was born prior to 1951, whose mother was Mabel Fred, sister of Matthew Fred. Mabel and Matthew are clan brother and sister of Roy's. When Mabel died, David courted Carmen. Carmen and David were not married when John was born. Roy told them to either get married, or he would take John and raise him as his own. They got married.

We have learned that it takes a great deal of patience to get information from Native people who might have the information a person might want. Roy has told me that it is not polite to directly ask the questions. (Being a white woman, I don't always heed that advice.) One must visit, and prove one's worthiness to have the information. It will also never (or seldom) be given, even by those people who know, if they are not the same clan as the person asking. We have finally learned quite a lot about Sophie from people who have become dear friends.

However, most of our inquiries about Roy's father have yielded very little information. We continue to be told "Don't worry about your father's story. The most important is your mother." This continues to bolster the matrilineal culture, but is difficult for Roy because he didn't know his mother, although he knew and loved his father dearly. We hope eventually we will learn some of the answers to questions we have. Why was Charlie Sr. adopted if he was an Aleut? Who adopted him and why? Was he a part of the Tlingit caste system? Did he have siblings? Were they adopted or blood? Was he born in Sitka? No one has ever volunteered anything and we do not know exactly where to begin. Recently Herman Kitka, *Kaagwaantaan* elder, told us that his grandfather and Roy's paternal grandfather were brothers! This is amazing information, but we must be respectful of it and carefully pray that additional information will be forthcoming. This kind of information is always very carefully given, and we understand and appreciate the honor of being privy to it.

CHAPTER FOUR

The Orphanage

oy remembers he and his father arriving, probably sometime in 1931 or 1932, at the Bethel Beach Children's Home in Juneau, which was run by two Scandinavian women of a strict and joyless Christian fundamentalist sect. Roy was told to go to the basement to play with the other children. When he was called upstairs for a meal, his father was gone, and he was told he was to stay right there. He was positive his father did not mean to leave him, and he grieved the entire time he was there. One day, he decided he needed to go looking for his father, so he bundled up his few possessions, and started down the road to find him. He walked for a long time until one of the older boys from the home found him and took him back.

At this orphanage, punishment for all infractions was the requirement of reading the Bible and memorizing various chapters and verses. The women who ran the orphanage were also apparently very difficult to please. I say "apparently" because of a story Roy told me one time. One of the two women was blind. Roy was instructed to mop the kitchen floor. He worked extremely hard to be sure it was very clean. When he reported that he had finished, the blind woman came into the kitchen, knelt down, and felt the floor. She told Roy it was too wet, that he should have removed more of the water. So the next time Roy was told to mop the floor, he worked diligently to be sure he did not leave it too wet. When he was finished, the blind woman again came in, knelt down to check the floor, and told Roy it was so dry that he must not have mopped it, thinking he could get away with it because she was blind. He was told to mop the floor again.

Roy's years in the orphanage were summed up in his words: "Each child had to find [his] way through life or fight for what [each] got, which wasn't much. In the orphanage, I looked out for those younger and smaller than me, which meant fighting their battles for them when needed." Roy continues, saying he became a "tough, stoic youngster now taking all the challenges as they came along, an exceptionally stout little boy more than able to take care of most situations as they came up." A leadership role was placed on him and he accepted it without question. Days and weeks and years melted into long days of learning about the Bible, memorizing endless passages, neither knowing what they meant, nor caring. He didn't understand that there were two different school systems: the public schools and the "Indian" schools. The two women who ran the "Home" insisted that all their children attend the public schools. The principal reluctantly allowed it. On one occasion, the principal (Floyd Dryden, after whom a school in Juneau is now named) came into the classroom and loudly asked Roy in front of all the children what nationality he was. Roy said he "didn't know what the word *nationality* meant," so he said he didn't know. Mr. Dryden snorted and said "Yes, you do," and left the room.

Some of the children in the Bethel Beach Children's Home whom Roy remembers were Henry Ozawa, Adelaide Bartness, Ellen Kavande, Mary Pete, and Mary Forney. The only one he has seen in adult years is Adelaide Bartness who became Adelaide Jacobs when she married Mark Jacobs Jr. in Sitka in 1949.

One summer, one of the older high school girls and Roy were taken by the blind lady to Skagway for the summer. The purpose of this excursion was to oversee a remodeling of some rooms upstairs in a Skagway building so that the building could be used as a hotel or inn. Why Roy was selected or why the lady from the Home was going to do this is not clear.

The building being renovated was across the street from one of the more rowdy clubs in Skagway. Dances and parties were held there every Saturday night, with the sound of music and voices getting louder as the night wore on. Some of the club's customers even danced in the street, holding their glasses or bottles. The sound of the partying and breaking glass almost always kept Roy awake.

He still remembers that summer as one of the happiest times of his life. A young Tlingit man and his wife took an interest in Roy. One day, they took him mountain climbing, which he enjoyed immensely. However, he never saw them again.

That summer, he found an old wrecked bicycle which he fixed up enough so that he could ride it. He was allowed great freedom to roam about, and Roy took advantage of that, even to the point of being soundly scolded and chased away by the famous and formidable Mrs. Harriet Pullen, who owned and operated the Pullen House, a hotel-boarding house. Roy's crime was riding across her yard on his bicycle. Mrs. Pullen started her Skagway career baking pies which she sold to the Gold Rush miners flocking through Skagway at the turn of the century.

The original plan in the trip to Skagway was that the older girl was to be sent back to Juneau before the blind lady and Roy, but that didn't happen, and at the end of the summer, all three returned to Juneau together.

(Roy and I had a glorious visit to Skagway in 1977 when we took our boat and explored there for a few days while Roy reminisced about that summer long past.)

One of Roy's lifelong loves was "born" in the orphanage. Children who had been good during the week were allowed to sit around the radio on Sunday afternoon while classical music was played. Roy developed a love of classical music, and how to distinguish the various instruments that has stayed with him to this day. He loves music; he loves listening to the Russian Orthodox choir as they sing *a capella*. Music of all kinds has been one of Roy's passions. He has especially enjoyed finding recordings of indigenous music during our travels around the world. One of his beloved CDs is from a Bolivian group who played at an open-air restaurant in Boulogne, France, when we were there in 1994.

Clothing and shoes worn by all the children in the orphanage came from donations. One year when a large donation of shoes arrived, all the children found shoes they were able to wear. However, there was nothing that fit Roy's high wide feet except for a pair of girl's sandals. With no alternative in sight, Roy ended up wearing that pair of shoes the entire school year.

Roy's connection to the preparation of food is one that includes much teasing and laughter in our family, as he tells about the catastrophes he had when he got near a kitchen. One time in the orphanage, taffy was made and the grubby boys were allowed to help "pull the taffy." The story according to Roy: "[We] boys were more than enthusiastic to help with that. Amazing how that pure white taffy began to take on a faint grey color and later turned a deeper grey. Finally when it was deemed that enough pulling had been accomplished, the taffy had a shiny grey hue to it. Didn't matter to us boys, as we ate with gusto."

He also remembers the girls making Hot Cross Buns at Easter time. The boys were not allowed near the kitchen, but they were given one hot cross bun for breakfast and one for lunch, and then they thought about how good they were until they got them again the following Easter. He believes those buns were the reason he is so fond of the Easter bread that the ladies of the Russian Orthodox Church in Sitka make and frequently sell for Easter. Today's Easter bread has candied fruit and nuts in it, which makes it even more delicious. The frosting is like that on the Hot Cross Buns Roy remembers from his orphanage days.

CHAPTER FIVE

Subsistence

The Native community was and is still directly tied to the subsistence life style. Hunger was a real and present entity unless the family was willing and able to secure most of one's food from the land.

A food source seldom used today was seagull eggs. Large colonies of gulls would pick islands with very steep cliffs for nesting. Getting on the cliff from a boat bouncing in the ocean swells was a challenge in itself. Because of this, young men were depended upon to scale the cliff and gather the eggs. It was important to always leave one or two eggs in each nest to insure the continuation of the gulls. This rule was followed religiously. The gathered eggs would then be distributed to all the families involved in their gathering. Roy doesn't remember any difference in taste between gull eggs and "store bought" eggs. They were smaller but tasted good.

Another food to mention at this point is fermented salmon eggs. I don't know any Native peoples alive today who will say they like to eat them, but when I first came to Alaska there were a few: Emma Duncan and Sarah Hanbury come to mind. Neither Roy nor I know the method used to preserve the salmon eggs, but it seemed to me to be a food easily left behind as the culture changed. In the late 70's, mention of them would bring large gales of laughter from the group and comments about who really liked to eat them. However, this food was used as a bodily cleansing agent. A story was told to us by Bertha Karras from years ago about a white doctor and a little white boy who had a tape worm. The doctor had tried many techniques to rid the child of the tape worm and they had all failed. One day, he went to the Village and asked if there were Native remedies used for this purpose. He was told to have the boy eat the fermented salmon eggs. The doctor did so, and the boy was completely rid of the tape worm.

Seaweed, however, is still much prized by the Tlingits. There are only a few places where it can be gathered, and the process of preparation is lengthy and detailed. One kind used is called "black seaweed," and is gathered by the Tribe and by Littlefield's Dog Point Fish Camp. It is eaten with relish at ceremonial gatherings and probably in homes of those who still know how to prepare it. There is a recipe for seaweed soup cooked with salmon eggs which we've never tasted, but we have received reports of it being a well-liked dish.

Herring season occurred in the spring, along with gathering eggs. Herring were good food and were gathered by the use of herring rakes. This was a long, generally flat pole, with many nails along one edge which, when sliced through the water in the midst of the schools of herring, would bring in several fish with one swipe. The long flat pole resembled a long, slim, bladed oar. Herring were dried and/or smoked in the same manner as salmon.

When the salmon came back to the rivers to spawn in the fall, the older boys and young men got their long poles outfitted with gaff hooks so they could catch the salmon as they were headed up the river. The poles were twelve feet or more in length. Sufficient salmon had to be caught to supply the family for the winter.

Attention is drawn to the fact that already at this time in history, families were the unit to be supplied, as opposed to clans. Families tried to be self-sufficient and to take care of each other. It was important in the culture to take care of the widows and single parents. Because this is no longer done as carefully, and there are those who are falling through the cracks, it is good to note that Sitka Tribe's present policy to go hunting and fishing and thus supply the elders and needy with food gathered is bringing back the communal sharing and caring for the elders that is such an important part of the culture. It has been a wonderful blessing for Roy, since he no longer is able to gather; due to the generosity of the Tribe, we have herring eggs, deer meat, and salmon.

We gather berries, and I have learned about a few of the other foods of the land which are greatly prized by the Tlingit people. The salmon eggs were generally saved during the fall salmon harvest, but the rest of the viscera were discarded. Most of the fish to be used later in the year was dried on racks. People cut the fish heads off, (these were baked and eaten separately or boiled with seaweed), and then split the fish lengthwise, keeping the tails intact so they could be draped over the racks for drying. Roy speaks of the "art" of cutting the fish for the racks in the "newspaper" style for large fish, keeping the fish all in one piece that could be folded out on the racks and then folded back up afterwards. Because of the wet climate, the racks usually had to be brought back into the house to complete the drying process. Sockeye is also a favorite. Some consider a favorite way to fix sockeye is by half drying it and then baking it with potatoes and seal oil. The fish used the most was the "humpy," (the pink or humpback salmon), because it was so plentiful in Sitka.

When one hears the term "dry fish," any kind of fish could be made into dry fish, but humpy (humpback salmon) was the most frequently used. When I think of dry fish, I think of very thinly sliced fish dried to where it is almost crumbly in texture and sometimes almost transparent. "Newspaper dried fish" is similar to jerky. I have seen it only occasionally in today's food, even when a big feast is prepared for the public and listed as "Indian food" for tasting. It is undoubtedly difficult to prepare and is carefully shared.

Herring eggs were gathered in the spring in the same manner that's used today. The laying of hemlock branches in the water attracts the herring spawn which clings to the branches. The branches with the eggs on them are brought in to preserve the eggs to eat all winter, and used as currency for trade. As the people of Klukwan used hooligan (eulachon) oil for trade, so did the people of Sitka use herring eggs. Herring eggs were a tremendously sought-after commodity and delicacy of the Native peoples. Many years ago, they were dried for winter use, while currently they are frozen, usually with the branches intact. When the herring eggs were dried, the eggs could be soaked or heated in water which caused them to regain their crunchy texture, part of the allure of the taste.

Many people use the herring eggs for salads, casseroles, and other recipes, but the primary use is strictly as a dish by themselves. Some people like them raw. They are served on branches cut small enough to be served on plates, where one peels the eggs off the branches to eat, discarding the branches as one would discard crab or clam shells or other seafood shells. Personally, I have learned that the best way of "cooking" them, as they are easily overcooked, is to put them in a clean sink, and pour fresh boiling water over them. Then with a pair of scissors, it is easy to cut the branches small enough to fill plates and serve them. The only condiment necessary is soy sauce, which some people relish. If available, seal oil or hooligan oil is prized to eat with the herring eggs. Hooligan oil is the oil rendered from the eulachon fish in the Klukwan-Haines area of Southeast Alaska. Historically, the Tlingit were warriors and entrepreneurs, using both the herring eggs and hooligan oil as currency, with trade routes hundreds of miles both north and south.

In the early days of white domination of the various fisheries in the State of Alaska, companies paid for herring by the ton to be used for fertilizer. Roy tells of the entire Sitka Sound being white with herring spawn. Native peoples have been very worried about the state of the herring fishery, and whether the sac roe fishery (where the females are killed and the sac containing the roe is removed) was depleting the resource. As contrasted with salmon, herring live to spawn again. Almost 100% of the sac roe fishery product goes to Japan. At one time, Sitka Tribe tried to have a moratorium placed on the sac roe fishery, but with the enormous number of dollars involved, it was not to be. The Tribe then changed tactics, arguing for better "dispersal" of the fishery so as to continue to allow subsistence users the ability to gather herring eggs.

In 2000, the commercial roe fishery was opened only in those areas near Sitka where subsistence took place. Many subsistence users got no herring eggs at all because the commercial fishery interfered, and it was a sad year for the Native peoples. One interesting fact Sitka Tribe discovered that year, with still no acknowledgment by the State Fish and Game to date, is that the water (that year) might have been white with milt but there were no eggs spawned, indicating that the males were active, but not the females.

The Tribe then became very politically active in learning how to present the dilemma to the powers that be in the State of Alaska. They got the issue on the Fish and Game agenda at a meeting late in 2000, an unheard-of happening. It took many months of very hard work, but the "dispersal" suggestion was accepted, and the Tribe is now supposed to be a part of the decision process when the location of the commercial sac roe fishery is determined.

Slowly but surely, the Native peoples of Alaska are learning how to make their voices heard in the white man's way. They have learned how to use the white man's processes better than the white man, in order to protect the Native peoples and their resources.

Fish (herring, salmon, and halibut, as well as clams, gumboots [chiton], and cockles), venison, and seal meat were smoked for preservation for winter. In the smokehouse, the meat was smoked hard like jerky so that it would keep through the winter. Families kept their own recipes for brine; these recipes varied from family to family. Each family had their own smoke house, and frequently, it was the young children who had to stay up day and night and keep the fire fed with just the right amount of green alder wood to keep the meat in the smoke. Roy says that was hard work for small children.

Herring eggs were also dried for winter, as were berries. In the summer and fall, everyone would be busy day and night to make sure there was sufficient food to last throughout the winter. Fish camps still existed, but there were fewer of them than in the 19th century, although there were still stories and areas claimed for this purpose. The best source of information about this is in *Haa Aaní, Our Land*, which was first issued in 1946 as a federal government Indian land claims document titled *Possessory Rights of the Natives of Southeastern Alaska*. It provides information as to the locations and uses of the land. It was written by Walter Goldschmidt and Theodore Haas, and was reprinted in 1998 by Sealaska Heritage Foundation with an introduction by Thomas Thornton, original Native witness statements, and a reminiscence by Walter Goldschmidt.

Herring eggs were the currency of the Native peoples of Sitka for millennia. They were used to acquire tanned moose hide, a valued clothing source, and hooligan (eulachon) oil, along with other prized items from other areas. Even today, when asked where they get their herring eggs, Natives from around the State and in the lower 48 will always say, "Sitka."

Charlie Sr. and Roy frequently went hunting together during his Sheldon Jackson years and beyond. His father taught him how to make a deer call with leaves. Charlie used very rough leaves for this, but Roy taught himself how to make a call using smoother leaves. Most Native men make deer calls from various leaves. Roy learned how to do this simply by being with his father or another older man.

When hunting, his father would always stop for a prayer to thank the deer for their giving of life so the family could eat. Roy learned that he himself loved these beautiful outdoors, and he learned always to give thanks beforehand for the bounty. Without the food brought to Charlie's home from hunting or fishing, there was nothing to eat. Roy's brother Charlie was a superb marksman, and Roy was impressed with his abilities. Their father always said there was no need for more than one bullet per deer, so Roy carried two bullets and a sandwich inside his shirt whenever he went out for food for the table. Roy tells of the time his brother, from about 200 feet, shot a buck between the eyes with such precision that the bullet, from the large caliber gun his brother carried, peeled the skull back so that it was hanging by the hide at the neck.

After Roy left school at the end of his sophomore year of high school, he preferred going hunting by himself. If there was not an urgent need for food, he found himself sitting under a tree and just watching the wildlife and the scenery. He took up his father's preferences of leaving before dawn and arriving on the hunting grounds just before the sun came up. Roy was surprised when I asked him how he could see to hike in the dark. He said, "I don't know. I knew the country." The places I have heard him talk about hunting included Indian River Valley, Verstovia Mountain, the mountains around Katlian Bay, and the mountains around Deep Inlet.

Roy climbed Verstovia several times as a boy, sometimes with school mates, racing up the mountain at three in the afternoon and then running down as the sun set, trying to get back to Sheldon Jackson School before they missed the evening meal. Frequently, the hike began up Indian River Valley where the decision was made to climb Verstovia from that direction. In order to get down the mountain in the winter darkness, the boys would turn down the tops of their rubber boots so that they could see the white on the boots of the boy ahead as they hurried down the mountain so as not to miss their dinner. His father would shake his head and say, "It's a wonder you stayed alive." In spite of this, Roy was saddened by Native hunters who went into the hills to hunt, and slipped and fell to their deaths. The mountains are steep and dangerous, and need to be as highly respected as the sea. He learned the lifelong respect and caution he holds for Nature and the wilderness that is the outdoors of Sitka, Alaska.

Besides berries, there were other foods such as beach asparagus; Roy vaguely remembers this delicacy but not well enough to know how it was gathered and preserved. He does remember eating nettles in the orphanage. They sting like crazy if a person bumps into them in the woods. A Norwegian carpenter with very thick skin on his hands picked them for the orphanage. Roy says that thick skin protected him from the sting. He thought nettles tasted something like spinach, but he has never eaten them anywhere other than the orphanage, so he doesn't know if this is a traditional food of the Native people, or if it is of some other ethnicity.

This subsistence lifestyle speaks to how the Tlingit culture is tied to the sea, or "sea-born" as Roy has always called the people. The sea provided most of their food and some of their clothing. It was important to have access to a boat for fishing and hunting or both.

Lydia George told us about the following event. As I understood her, as well as Jimmy George and Harold Jacobs telling me about the same occasion, the story goes like this: When Angoon (*Killisnoo*) was shelled in 1882 by the U.S. Navy, all of the canoes were destroyed but one. The one canoe that was not destroyed was owned by the *Deisheetaan* of *Deishú hít*. The prow of this canoe is all that is left today. It has been recently repatriated, a beautiful, carved beaver, and is now part of treasured *at.óow* of *Deishú hít* .

As I understand what happened, *Gaaxwéi*, from Sitkoh Bay, was the caretaker of that canoe and the beautiful beaver prow. His nephew, John Paul, (Roy's maternal grandfather) was a teenager at the time of the bombardment. He had asked his uncle if he could use the canoe. He wanted to fish, or hunt, or look for something that morning. It is not important what the purpose was; John Paul and the canoe

PI-083   *Collection,*
about 1900.

The beaver prow shown in picture above repatriated and in possession of the Deisheetaan of Angoon

were fortuitously not at the village when the U.S. Navy shelled *Killisnoo*.

In his most interesting essay, "The Day We Paid for a Crime We Didn't Commit," Harold Jacobs writes, "One canoe survived the bombardment, and I heard those stories from the time I was able to  off to my grandparent's

direct descendent caretaker of that canoe, and he has given us essay. He was stunned w ognized, the canoe prow ural History in New York tion process, long and laborious culminated in great celebration. The

tic

That boat had to procure all the food for the whole village

of

caretakers of the canoe prow is as follows: After *Gaaxwéi* of Sitkoh Bay, John Paul (*Kootla.aa*) became its caretaker and after him Charlie John, *Took*, became caretaker." Today's *Gaaxwéi*, Jimmy George, is the caretaker of that canoe prow.

Once again quoting from Harold's essay, "Very little escaped destruction...... Six children were killed in the bombardment.........If it wasn't for that one canoe, Angoon probably wouldn't exist today as it does, a stronghold of Tlingit culture, with about a dozen of its seventeen clan houses still standing..... [rebuilt after the bombardment] The *Deisheetaan* have eight houses; the *L'eeneidí* have two houses, the *Dak'laweidí* have three houses, the *Wooshkeetaan* have three houses, and the *Teikweidí* have two houses. Of these, fourteen of the structures are still standing and most are still occupied [today]."

This web site http://www.uscg.mil/history/**WEBCUTTERS/** Corwin1876.html in the Coast Guard historical archives has an account of this happening. This is a portion of the information found there and quoted in Harold's essay:

"In October 1882 a Northwest Trading Company whaleboat chased a whale into the waters near the Tlingit Indian Village of Angoon, on Kootznahoo Inlet, Admiralty Island. The whaling gun aboard exploded, killing *Tith Klane*, a Tlingit shaman who worked for the company. The other natives aboard the whaling boat took two company employees E. H. Bayne and S. S. Stulzman, who were also crewmen on the boat, hostage in an effort to extract payment from the company for the death of their shaman. They landed at Angoon. There they, along with the villagers, sought payment of 40 blankets.

"A company representative sought the assistance of the

only naval warship in the area, the crew from the screw frigate *USS Adams,* under the command of a Commander Merriman, which was tied up at Sitka. As the *Adams* drew too much water to get close to Angoon, Merriman sought and obtained the assistance of Healy and the *Corwin,* which was in Sitka at the time obtaining coal. Healy agreed and the *Corwin,* with Merriman and 50 sailors and 20 marines from *Adams* aboard, set sail on 24 October 1882, apparently towing the Company's tug *Favorite* along with the *Adams'* launch, to the waters off Angoon. Merriman had armed the *Favorite* with a small howitzer and Gatling gun.

"According to the official history of the *Adams* "Upon arrival at Angoon, the force collected as many of the Indians' canoes as possible, and Comdr. Merriman held a meeting with some of the Indians during which he made counter demands for the release of the hostages and a levy of 400 blankets in return for which the expedition would spare their canoes and village. To buy time, the Indians accepted the demands at first and released the hostages; however, after they had an opportunity to hide their canoes and gather their forces, the Indians refused to honor the agreement. Thereupon, *Corwin* and *Favorite* took the village under fire, destroying a number of houses. When the ships ceased fire, a landing party went ashore and set fire to some of the remaining houses. At that point, the Indians submitted. Comdr. Merriman left a party of sailors at Angoon to insure continued good faith, and he and the remainder returned to Sitka in *Corwin* to re-embark in *Adams.*

"Apparently six children suffocated when the village's houses were put to the torch and the villagers suffered greatly that winter, having lost their means of livelihood in the canoes and their shelter from the weather."

Harold continues, "According to Steve Henrickson, Curator of Collections at the Alaska State Museum, a letter was found in 1989 in a garbage dump by a man named Karl Lemmerman. Eventually winding up in the collection of Yale's Beinecke Library (Juneau Empire, 8/12/99), it turns out that this letter was written by a crew member believed to be Frank H. Clark of the *USS Adams.* The letter excerpt is as follows:

"Lt. Bartlett went on a steam tug belonging to the North West Trading Co. He took besides his sixty men and rifles a howitzer and Gatling gun. All this preparation against a lot of Indians half of whom were unarmed.

"On their arrival at *Hoochenoo* (later called Angoon) the Indian village where the property was seized, they found the two white men released and the property all restored.

"The Captain then notified the Indians that they must pay him four hundred blankets as a penalty for their unlawful conduct and gave them until the next day at noon to raise them. The next morning, they had raised only a little over a hundred, and at noon only one hundred and twenty [sic] he then burned and bombarded a few houses that were at our side of the village and at the same time raised his demand to 800 blankets which is $2,400.

"This they did not comply with and he then gave orders to shell the town. After firing thirty or forty shells into the town, he sent the sailors and marines and burned about forty houses, some of which cannot be replaced for $3,000 and only left five houses standing.

"Besides the dwellings there were a large number of storehouses filled with smoked salmon and other winter supplies. All this was burned too.

"Many of the Indians were away at Harrisburg (later called Juneau) mining and their houses contained everything they possessed and were all burned up. Of course those Indians who were there, saved what they could before the burning.

"Mr. Vanderbilt who is prejudicial against the Indians estimated the loss to the tribe at 30 or 40 thousand dollars. This of course does not include the suffering to women and children who will suffer from want of shelter and food during the winter. As the weather there is much more severe than here it will undoubtedly cause much suffering.

"Most of the officers including myself consider it a brutal and cowardly thing and entirely uncalled for. It would have been well enough to have arrested the ringleaders and punished them, but in this case many innocent people suffered more than the guilty, and a large number of them helpless women and children. It is estimated that there are about 800 people in the village.

"We are all anxious to see the account the papers

will give of it and the report the Capt. will give of it. In other words, how big a lie he will tell in order to justify himself."

Harold finishes the essay with this information: "*Til'tlein,* the *ixt'* (shaman) whose death precipitated the bombardment was *Deisheetaan.* His direct descendants today [are] the children, grandchildren and great-grandchildren of [Robert and] Helen James, Paul [and Isabelle James] Chulik and Tommy [and Josephine Nakamura] Chulik.

The destruction of the village by the U.S. Navy was a travesty that should never have happened, but it is still alive in the hearts and minds of the Angoon people as though it happened last week. This trauma may never be forgotten. Although requested many times by many people, including Governor Jay Hammond, an apology has never been given.

When Roy was a boy, the round-bottom, double-ended row boat was the boat of choice. These boats were used for transportation and trolling for salmon. Some of these boats were locally built; others were imports which were built with oak ribs and Port Orford cedar planking fastened with copper fasteners. These boats would glide through the water with a minimum of effort.

About this same time, seine skiffs were making their presence known. Humpies, sockeyes, kings, chum, and silvers were being seined; however, sockeyes and kings brought the best prices. These fish were brought into canneries which were located up and down Southeast Alaska, where thousands of tons of these fish were put into cans and sent south. The seine skiffs were flat-bottomed, heavy, clumsy boats, but they were built for heavy use and were able to take considerable punishment and keep afloat.

Fishing for salmon was a simple arrangement. A cotton braided line a couple of hundred feet long was tied to a four to eight pound lead sinker. The line was fastened to a short stout stick on the gunwale of the boat as it was rowed along in the water. Therefore, it got the name of hand trolling!

Roy and his father went on several excursions in this manner, with camp being made ashore every night for cooking purposes. Roy's story: "One time on one trip, we heard an annoyed bear growling around through the woods. So that night, we slept in the boat anchored away from shore. During the trolling, the oar locks, being made of metal, made noise as the boat was rowed. To quiet the squeaking and clanking of the rowing motion, we put pieces of rags between the metal parts. Don't remember getting rich in that effort. Another time in fall of the late 1930's or early 40's, Dad had gone hunting out past old Sitka Rock. At that time of the year, the weather is unpredictable, and on his way back to Sitka, coming along an area that was called Dragon Tooth Rock, he was too close to the shore and a breaking wave caught his boat, turned it upside down, and rolled it up on the shore. He lost everything in the surf, including his glasses. The next day, my Dad, brother and I went out to look for the glasses and any other items of value. My brother found the glasses and all seemed to return to normal. Today that same area is where the surfers congregate when the surf is up."

Transportation throughout Southeast Alaska was always more difficult than it was in areas connected by roads. There was no ferry service back then, and Alaska Steamship Company had regular but infrequent service. Earlier, there was a small boat called the *Estebeth*, which Roy says the kids called "the mail boat." It carried mail, freight, and a few passengers between Juneau and Sitka. After the era of the *Estebeth*, the Northland Company entered the market with two vessels. *The North Sea* was the largest, and the smaller one was called the *Northland;* after them the Alaska Steamship Company took over with larger vessels and more regular service to Sitka. It was on the Northland Company ships that Roy did his orphanage-days trips to and from Sitka. And, of course, there was no regularly scheduled commercial air service then.

The beginnings of what would become Alaska Airlines were taking place, but air travel was primarily by the Grumman Goose operated by Alaska Coastal Airlines, which landed on the water, and then taxied up to "the ramp" in front of what is now the University of Alaska and Mt. Edgecumbe High School. By then, Mt. Edgecumbe High School had opened for students from all over Alaska, and sometimes there might be five or six Grumman Goose delivering students or picking them up to fly them home to their respective villages. The locals called it the "brown-eyed airlift." When Mt.

Edgecumbe High School opened, all the students at Wrangell Institute were transferred to Sitka, and the Wrangell Institute was closed.

CHAPTER SIX

Third Grade

The summer before Roy began second grade in 1934, Charlie married Olinda Search, a *Kiks.ádi* widow who had been living in Hoonah. Olinda was at least ten years his senior. Here again, from bits and pieces of information told to us by different people over the years, we suspect a clan decision regarding this marriage union. Charlie really wanted his children home, and needed a wife in order to accomplish that. Olinda had a son to take care of and needed a husband for a provider. It is easy to imagine the *Chookaneidí* and the *Kiks.ádi* clan leaders making a strong suggestion that the answer to this dilemma was marriage. In any event, Roy was bundled up in 1935 with his small paper bag of belongings, an envelope pinned inside his coat, put on a Northland Company boat, and sent to Sitka. Roy was suddenly faced with a culture and language which had been washed out of him with laundry soap.

When we finally managed to secure enough evidence for the State of Alaska to issue a delayed certificate of birth for Roy, it included school records from the Juneau Public Schools. This covers 1st, 2nd, 4th, 5th, and 6th grades. The entire 3rd grade is missing. That is the year Roy spent in Sitka.

The new school was the Indian School that existed on the site of the Community House – *Sheet'ka Kwaan Naakahídi*. School seemed to be easy for Roy since he says everything taught there he had already learned in the Juneau Public School. He has very little memory about school itself, other than he didn't like it because he felt it was a waste of time, and he wished he could be learning something useful.

Carmen and Charlie Jr. were not living at home; Roy does not know where they were during that year. Olinda's son, Ronald Search, was living there. Ronald was about ten years older than Roy, a bully who enjoyed "alcohol and women." Roy was expected to keep the wood chopped for the stove which provided their heat and cooking. One time, the axe slipped, and Roy almost cut his thumb off. It was hanging by little more than skin. Olinda wrapped it up in a handkerchief and sent Roy by himself to the "nurse's house," where he sat and waited for a couple of hours before she came home and could attend to his thumb. By then, it was too late to do any stitching, and this woman simply taped up his thumb and sent him home. There was no other medical care available. This nurse was employed in the Pioneer's Home, which was the old military barracks located where the current Pioneer Home was built in 1933-34. The "nurse's house" was located near the current Kettleson Library next to the old "Double O" house.

The summer before he was sent back to the orphanage, he spent at Todd Cannery where Olinda and Charlie were working. He spent the summer in the company of the George Howard Sr. children. He remembers it being a fairly happy time. They would all go down to the beach at low tide, build a small fire, dig clams, and put them in the fire. He remembers how good those steamed clams were and how much fun he had with the Howard boys.

Olinda had developed a dislike for Roy, and she finally convinced Charlie that Roy should be sent back to the orphanage because he was "not Indian enough." According to Roy, her comment to him was, "You make a bad white man and a worse Indian." Roy had a difficult time coping with the food, or lack of it, the language which he had forgotten, the use of alcohol by all the members of the household, and the school which didn't teach him anything he didn't already know. So sometime in 1935, Roy was put on another Northland Company ship, and sent back to the Bethel Beach Children's Home.

CHAPTER SEVEN

Sheldon Jackson School

Roy finished 6th grade in 1939, and permanently left the Bethel Beach Children's Home and moved to Sitka to attend and live at Sheldon Jackson School, a Presbyterian School which had many of the rules and regimentation one would expect in such an environment. However, after Roy's experience in the Bethel Beach Home, he felt he had just been given his freedom from jail. He did not find the restrictions at Sheldon Jackson difficult or cumbersome, and he mostly enjoyed his time there. There were some adjustments, however. He could not understand why the boys would want to "go to town" when they did not have a specific objective in doing so. He had certainly never gone to town, other than with a specific purpose to accomplish. He had never been to a movie. He had never seen dancing or been to a dance. He had never had an opportunity to hear popular music. He had never played cards. He had never done anything on Sunday other than go to church. He had never read anything for pleasure. So now he enjoyed the new freedom to explore the outdoors, and he "mostly" enjoyed the classes.

Playing in the Village – this is the earliest picture we have of Roy, probably taken about 1937

An interesting phenomenon existed in Sitka at the turn of the 19th century. Natives in Sitka were from two camps: the Village and the Cottages. Those who lived in the Village lived a more traditional life style in what shows on current plats and maps as the Indian Village in Sitka. It is that part of town which fronts on Katlian Street. (It used to be known as "The Ranche" during Russian times.) It was the part of town that was kept separate from downtown Sitka by the Russians with a fort-like fence. In those days, Indians were not allowed into town after dark, and the gate could be closed against those who lived in the Village.

Many living in the Village were members of the Russian Orthodox Church.

Tlingits who lived in the Cottages, located on the eastern side of Sheldon Jackson School where the Sitka National Historical Park is now located, were the group of Indians who became mostly Presbyterians. There are houses on Metlakatla Street and Kelly Street that remain from the Cottages era. There was a great deal of competition between the Village and the Cottages that spilled over into life at SJ.

Roy remembers that both the Village and the Cottages had their own bands. He doesn't know whether band members could read music, but they could certainly make wonderful music, and play they did at any opportunity.

The Village, being primarily Russian Orthodox, and the Cottages, being primarily Presbyterian, led to another interesting cultural issue. The Russian Orthodox Church came to Alaska with priests who learned the Tlingit language and customs, married the Tlingit women, and lived within the society that existed here. In the same breath, they converted the Indian people to the Orthodox religion, and adapted the culture into the church's rites and theology. There were many things in the Native culture that easily slid into Russian Orthodox Christianity. This church also accepted for priesthood Native men without requiring that they give up all their culture and customs.

*Sitka National Historical Park - Merrill Collection
Sitk3916 "The Village, Sitka, Alaska"*

*"The Cottages", photographed by Louis Shotridge, University
of Pennsylvania Museum, No. 15122" - Olinda Baileys
mother's house is the one on the far right.*

The Presbyterians, on the other hand, required anyone wanting to become a minister to go to seminary and complete college. Many of these were the men who wore the "three piece suit." Roy has always considered himself Presbyterian. The first Native man to become a Presbyterian minister was Walter Soboleff. In his 90's now, he is a much beloved elder of the Tlingit people.

Of course, there were many other Christian churches that Natives attended. Some of these date back to the late 19th century, but the ones which seemed to have had the most influence on Native lives appeared to be the Presbyterian and the Russian Orthodox, the latter sometimes referred to in historical archives as Greek Orthodox.

When Roy and I lived on Biorka Island in the mid 1970's, and were able to get Charlie and Olinda out there one time for a visit, Charlie reminisced about Biorka and visitors from Sitka coming into what is now known as Symonds Bay. Seamen aboard visiting boats always had their own musical instruments. They would quietly enter the bay and then start playing for the surprised people on shore. Then those on shore would get their own instruments and would come down to the beach, playing to welcome them. Music was very much a much beloved part of everyone's life. The traditional back and forth oratory would ensue before those on the boat(s) would come ashore. Charlie also said that Biorka's sand beach was called a sugar sand beach because it looked like sugar; it was fine and white. This proves to me that many of the larger islands were inhabited by the

Native peoples even through the beginning of the 20th century, something that has been disputed for many years.

Olinda's mother's house was in the Cottages, located approximately where the path from the upper parking lot at the Sitka National Historical Park starts down to the Visitor Center level. Charlie's house was in the Village. Roy, therefore, had a foot in both camps, which made life at SJ challenging. He certainly had acquired a "journeyman's license" in knowing how to fight and protect himself from those who wanted to challenge his credentials as a genuine Tlingit. The first shock he encountered was that many of his classmates were bigger and tougher than any he had met in Juneau. As he says, "They were able to mop the floor with me, much to my surprise and chagrin." At first he thought of revenge and explained to each that someday he would "get" them. Roy and the other boys finally accepted the fact that everyone, including Roy, had exceptional strength, and perhaps it would be better to leave well enough alone.

This furthered Roy's journey into introspection and "being a loner," even though my personal take on it is that Roy is much more gregarious and social than he admits. Perhaps that's because there has been healing in his later years. He joined some of the other boys who had recently arrived at Sheldon Jackson, and they found themselves with similar interests exploring this new country from one end to the other. One of their continuing adventures was to take a jump into the flume the first thing every morning. The flume receives water from Indian River and meanders across the Sheldon Jackson campus like a lovely natural stream. This water went down to the power plant through an underground pipe, and furnished power for the school's electric generator. Frigid icy water in November was a brisk initiation into the boyhood fraternity of school mates.

Roy calls his 7th and 8th grade years "our Tom-Sawyer-type-happy-go-lucky-life" which, in spite of the occasional cultural clash, was what made this life at Sheldon Jackson so "free and happy." He thought of Sheldon Jackson as an exceptionally "free" place compared to the orphanage, and never could understand the complaints of classmates about the restrictions placed on them.

On weekends, he and his schoolmates would explore the Indian River valley. When they found "minnows" in the river in quiet pools, they would devise a way to "go fishing." Taking long stocks of dried grass about three feet long, they would dig up some earth worms, and tie them to the ends of the grass. Then they would dangle this fishing contraption into the water where the small fish would immediately clamp onto the worm and could be brought out of the water. I asked Roy what they did with the fish after they'd caught them. He looked at me like that was a very strange question and said, "Why, we ate them, of course!" They would build a fire on the river bank, and spear the fish and roast them. Soon, in the manner of boys everywhere, their boundless energy would take over, and they had to keep going on up the valley or up Verstovia Mountain. When dinner time was imminent, they would run headlong back down the valley to get home in time to eat.

At Sheldon Jackson School, there were several manual shops available to the boys: woodworking, machine, and print shops are the ones Roy remembers. He's often told me of operating the printing machine that now resides at Old Harbor Book Store. (The old printing press which is in the Sitka Historical Museum is much older, from the Russian era.) Apparently, he became quite adept at the typesetting, which required that a person read the words upside down and backwards. Girls were not necessarily forbidden from the manual shops, but the mores of the times prohibited them from taking manual shop classes.

School was interesting to Roy, but not many of the classes made any lasting impression upon him other than biology, which he found fascinating. He enjoyed learning about plant life, and when the subject of hydroponics came up, he found himself enthralled. He got a part time job with a man who was growing a hydroponics garden. In Roy's words, "Growing plants in just water caught my attention. How could this be? .... No dirt, or earth but just water and the mass of roots were clearly visible." However, this gentleman's attention turned from hydroponics to other matters, and Roy was out of a job and out of a place to learn more about this fascinating subject.

Sheldon Jackson tried to provide a bit of after school activity in the form of "socials." Boys at this age are almost always awkward. Roy had never had any opportunity in his life to socialize – a chance to visit and enjoy activities with girls. Many of these "socials" involved dancing. Once again in Roy's words, "My feet just did not cooperate and besides, how were you supposed to hold a girl?" He and his friends, however, discovered with amazement "how soft girls felt." Roy indicated that "many of the girls were accomplished dancers before coming to SJ." So "this was very embarrassing for us guys," who did not know how to dance. Dancing never became even a secondary interest to Roy whose only important indoor sport was basketball. He does tell of the fact that his father loved to dance, and frequently did so at the ANB Hall where dances were held regularly.

His four years at Sheldon Jackson, and the time after Roy left school before he was drafted, gave him many opportunities to get reacquainted with his father and brother. For the first time, he could spend time with them during the school year and summers. (Roy lived and ate his meals at the school, however). During this period, he was able to meet and conquer the cultural gap which, although still a shock, was just another of life's battles to fight and win. Many of his classmates became very special to him, although many were three to four years older than he was. He also renewed many connections from third grade.

There were two other people who had a big influence on Roy during his SJ days: Les Yaw, the head of the school, and Jeannie (Eugenie) Williams, a lifelong spinster from New York, who was in charge of the laundry. All of the adults at the school were white men and women who had come in a missionary spirit to work with the Indian children and help them become Christians. Some were more evangelical than others.

Jeannie, who eventually adopted an orphaned Tlingit boy from Hoonah whose name was Eddie Newton, took an interest in Roy. When he and Eddie went into her house, she always would give them saltine crackers with peanut butter on them – a delightful treat. When Roy and I moved to Biorka Island in 1975, and then to Sitka in 1978, Jeannie and Les Yaw were still in Sitka, and I was able to meet them and become friends. Les told me one time that he had always had high hopes for Roy's potential, and he was glad that Roy had gotten an education and had a successful career. When Jeannie died, Roy came home from the funeral and made himself a snack of saltine crackers with peanut butter on them in her honor.

Jeannie's son, Eddie, had died in a house fire years before, and his children did not acknowledge Jeannie as their grandmother. Roy and I were able to start a fund which eventually purchased a headstone for her grave. She is buried just down the hill from where Charlie and Olinda are buried in the old Sitka Cemetery. Roy spent a lot of time playing with Les Yaw's son, Robert. Robert was killed in a military accident while serving in the army in San Francisco during WWII, and is buried in the National Cemetery in Sitka.

Around 1979, I met Gladys Whitmore, one of the teachers from Roy's time. She was overjoyed to see Roy. She took my hand and said "He was one of the good boys, you know. I never realized how young he was in comparison to the others so I was much too hard on him." Roy certainly had a healthy respect for her (!), and possibly even a little affection.

It is interesting to note that during the years when Roy attended Sheldon Jackson School, he was able to develop a relationship with his father that lasted throughout the balance of Charlie Sr.'s life. He also had a chance to get to know his brother Charlie during that time, although not as well as he would have liked. Shortly after Roy returned home from the war, Charlie Jr. was sent to Cushman Hospital in Tacoma, Washington, to be treated for tuberculosis. Charlie, Jr. never returned, and the place where the hospital stood is now a cloverleaf on a freeway. Before the hospital was torn down to make way for the freeway, Roy tried to find his brother's grave, but the records had been kept on the back of an empty tablet written in pencil. Try as he did, he could not find his brother's name on the list, so the grave's location remains unknown.

Olinda came to trust Roy in her later years, although she never allowed herself any affection for him. She made him the caretaker of her extra money, and depended on him to be sure she received a "Christian burial."

As always, with dignity and respect, Roy did see to her final arrangements, made sure her burial place had a marker, and gave her remaining money to Ronald, keeping nothing for himself. Just a couple of years before Ronald died, he came to Sitka, and was amazed to see his mother's burial place with a beautiful bronze marker. He wanted to

know who had paid for it and Roy told him that he had.
Ronald was appreciative.

CHAPTER EIGHT

Boats and Boat Building

By the time Roy was in the 8th grade, he had become a tugboat operator. Don Cook, who was related in some way to Olinda, took Roy under his wing, and had him helping while they moved logs for Columbia Lumber Company. Eventually, Don acquired a second boat, and Roy ran the first one. The second boat Don Cook acquired was a sunken boat, washed up on a beach, to which Don took salvage rights. He repaired it and used it in the tugboat business that he and Roy operated. The tugboats replaced those men who used to move logs manually with long poles. They had frequent accidents and loss of life. Small boats with big engines could move those logs around safely and more efficiently. They would pick up the logs from the site, raft them, and take them to Camp Coogan Bay. From there, they brought them as needed to Columbia Lumber for sawing. Roy and Don did this from 1940 to 1942, when Samson Tug and Barge came into being, and started giving them so much competition that they were unable to keep going. Roy enjoyed running a tugboat immensely, and it was one reason he was able to get the job as a shore boat operator when he returned from the war.

The mission boat *SJS I* (*Sheldon Jackson School I*) was in existence when Roy first came to Sheldon Jackson. However, Roy has no information about how that boat came to be. Peter Simpson is the one usually attributed with building the *SJS I*, with student help. A boat was imperative for Sheldon Jackson School to have because they used it not only for transportation to and from the Southeast villages, but for subsistence. Most of their food was subsistence fish and venison secured by older students going out fishing and hunting on the *SJS I* and subsequent boats.

Soon the *SJS I* was considered too small to continue with the increasing transportation needs of the school as a whole. The Board of Missions decreed that a new boat needed to be built; therefore, the *Princeton Hall* came into existence. The first boat Roy remembers being built was the *Princeton Hall*. It was built in Andrew Hope's boat shop, also on Katlian Street, about where the Bellows' family has their airplane float presently. The *Princeton Hall* was large for its time. Princeton University was a large contributor to SJ and had continued to make donations to the school for operations; therefore, the name *Princeton*. The Hall

Family made a large specific donation for the building of the *Princeton Hall*; thus, the final name for the boat to be built. The *Princeton Hall* was to take the place of the *SJS I* for missionary work to the villages.

The building of the *Princeton Hall* was meticulous, with well-known naval architectural planning for the heavy and well-built yacht. Lumber was imported for the work: fir for the keel and some planking, oak for the ribs, with the deck beams being made of Alaska yellow cedar. The superstructure and pilot house were faced with mahogany. Special carpenters and master boat builders were brought in to work on the cabin's mahogany fittings, etc.

Students at SJ volunteered to work on this boat. It was not one of the required classes; the *Princeton Hall* was built during winter months when it was very cold and miserable. Pictures exist which show students working on the *Princeton Hall*. Sadly, Moses Johnson and Roy, who both spent many and regular hours working, were not present when any of these photos were taken. The bitter winter cold led both of them, on occasion, to have colds and be confined to the dormitories until they recovered. The boat shop was not heated and work continued in all weather and conditions with a great deal of enthusiasm. Roy and Moses Johnson worked on the *Princeton Hall* from the beginning to the end.

After all the planking was coated with cuprinol, which is a green-tinged, copper-based wood preservative, one of the boys' major jobs was caulking the planking with oakum down around the keel. I guess today's society would cringe at the idea of 14 and 15 year olds working with no protective clothing or special gloves, putting this compound on all the inside wooden planking. Oakum was very heavy, looking like sisal or hemp rope, although it was loose, not bound. A large area required the oakum. The oakum smelled like tar, and it might have been contained in burlap bags; it looked like burlap without being woven. Next the hull planking below the water line was caulked with special, coarse, cotton fluffs inserted via a caulking chisel and hammer. This cotton had to be installed so it would expand and seal all seams to make the boat water-tight.

This caulking was usually done by the master builders, not by the students, as it was specialized work and extremely important to the integrity of the finished vessel. Many of the master builders would come and go as their expertise was needed and used.

After caulking the hull with the planking in place, the boat was ready for the water, although necessary finishing touches were done before it was launched. All seams were puttied and sanded to an extremely smooth finish so that no seams were visible. Moses and Roy worked on this sanding for countless hours, continuing on into the building of the superstructure, and the pilot house. Towards the end, the entire hull was hand-sanded. Untold hours of sanding in the cold caused them to buy chewing gum, when they had the money, to counteract the dust in their noses and throats. Places of great challenge were the wooden plugs placed over the fasteners that held the planking to the boat. Once, Roy's chewing gum was placed in a knothole at the top of the bow stem. As far as Roy knows, that gum is still there and the story of its placement lives on!

The sealant used at that point was called the "first coat" of paint. Moses and Roy were exuberant and happy, applying their brushes vigorously. At one point, Roy was on scaffolding above Moses and the exuberance extended to the end of Moses' brush, as he reached up and made a swath of paint up between Roy's legs, where he was spread-eagled to keep his balance. It was a grand time of laughter, hard work, and horse play.

In Roy's words, "The *Princeton Hall* was as beautiful as a yacht should be." Launching day arrived with much excitement. Moses and Roy were there to observe the launching, but a sad and sobering situation had come about. The Coast Guard was there and took charge of the *Princeton Hall* before it was put in the water. They towed it away, and Roy didn't see it again but once in Icy Strait, where it was put to use as a Coast Guard patrol boat. The beautifully glistening, smooth, white finish was now battleship grey. A high-speed diesel engine had been put in the *Princeton Hall*. It was, Roy guessed, a 160hp super-charged engine which allowed the boat to cruise at about 15 knots, exceedingly fast for a vessel of that size. (The *Princeton Hall* was unpowered when it was towed away by the Coast Guard so the installation and description of the engines is a matter of conjecture.)

The *Princeton Hall* has been purchased by a couple in Juneau whose last name is Ruddy. They completely refurbished the *Princeton Hall,* and its history has been preserved and honored in several ways. We have attended, among other events, a special commemorative occasion in Angoon honoring the *Princeton Hall.* We have coffee mugs in honor of the occasion, given to the attendees by the current owners. We caught sight of the vessel in Juneau as recently as the spring of 2004, where it sits, shining and white as it was meant to be.

The following is a quote from a web page devoted to the *Princeton Hall* today:

> "The *MV Princeton Hall* is a 65' cruising yacht, USCG inspected and licensed. Her history is interesting and varied: built in Sitka, Alaska, in 1941, she was originally designed as a "mission boat" for the Presbyterian Church. Six days after [the day] she was launched, the US Navy [U.S. Coast Guard] conscripted the vessel to use as a patrol boat during WWII. She was sold back to the Church and resumed duties for the next 25 years as a mission boat to the remote communities of Southeast Alaska.
>
> "Now under private ownership and completely renovated from stem to stern, she is enrolled in the Classic Yacht Association. A tested and proven vessel, she has safely cruised the Inside Passage for almost

sixty years. Accommodations are hospitable and very comfortable for groups of six to eight guests. Her design provides a safe, stable, and functional vessel to enjoy your Alaskan adventure up close."

Whenever I have asked Roy who the "master boat builder" was who built the *SJS II*, he avoided the subject. The *SJS II* was built in George Howard's boat shop on Katlian Street using a design of Andrew Hope's. Some readers may remember a long article about the Howard boat shop in the <u>Daily Sitka Sentinel</u> at the time this shop was torn down a few years ago. Many members of the Howard family consider their father, George Howard Sr., to be the builder of the *SJS II* because it was built in their father's boat shop. Students of Sheldon Jackson School remember Andrew Hope being the "one who was always there" during the building of the *SJS II*. The Hope family believes their father, Andrew Hope, was the builder of the *SJS II* as well as the other famous mission boat, the *Princeton Hall*. This has caused many hard feelings and argument. I suspect it is primarily about semantics and I am sorry the controversy exists.

Only the *SJS I* and *SJS II* were used for subsistence. There was still a need for another boat after the *Princeton Hall* was taken for military use. I am guessing the order from the Board of Missions to build another boat took place about 1940. Sitka had already been taken over by the military approximately a year earlier, as the U.S. government was concerned about the possibility of war with Japan because of the latter's provocative posturing. On those trips, the school choir sometimes went to provide music. There was much comment by many people regarding the quality of Native voices raised in song. Roy was a member of the SJ choir but never went with the choir on any trips in any of the boats.

Sheldon Jackson School was in a quandary – they still were in desperate need of a boat to provide transportation. Through some machinations unknown to Roy or any of the students, they were allowed to build, keep, and use another boat which became the *SJS II* on which Moses and Roy also worked many long hours.

The *SJS II* was built entirely by local Native master boat builders using local design and methods with similar construction materials as the *Princeton Hall* (although Roy has never mentioned any deposited gum on the *SJS II*). The Board of Missions got hold of an old diesel engine, a 60hp medium speed marine Atlas diesel engine. It was extremely heavy and chugged along at about 100 rpm.

The launch of the *SJS II* was planned to coincide with the arrival of the *Alaska Steamship*, which tied up at Conway Dock. The *SJS II* was towed alongside of the steamship, and the heavy diesel engine was hoisted into the *SJS II*. The *SJS II* was a bit bigger than the run-of-the-mill seine boats of that time. The boat was then towed away to have the engine retrofitted and ready to go while the students, especially Roy and Moses, continued to work on the sanding and painting. A seine was loaded aboard along with a seine skiff that had been built especially for the purpose. While they were still painting the superstructure, the boat left Sitka to go to Tenakee Inlet to fish. While painting the turn-table (used for appropriately arranging the seine when pulling it in by hand – no longer needed in these days of using hydraulics) in Tenakee, the work on the boat was finally terminated for the summer, when the fishing began.

Roy worked on the *SJS II* all summer, seining from Tenakee to Icy Strait as the season went along. From Icy Strait, the fishing continued on down to Craig and Klawock. This constituted a period of time from approximately March through September.

Roy remembers at the end of this time that he had earned approximately $300. He was not impressed with the pay scale. However, from this point on, he was in demand for boat work. He continued fishing over several summers as a crew member for Pete Nielson and Don Cook, among others. He was totally at home around boats and on the sea. He knew how they were built and why, he knew nautical language, could tie knots, read charts, and anchor and steer as well as having the knowledge necessary to seine. He was, in a manner of speaking, an able-bodied seaman.

CHAPTER NINE

World War II

All extracurricular activities at Sheldon Jackson came abruptly to an end on December 7, 1941, when the Japanese bombed Pearl Harbor. "When we saw the newsreels and pictures in the newspaper of the destruction the Japanese did in Hawaii, it left a very bitter taste in our mouths," Roy said to me when explaining what happened in Sitka. The military had come to Sitka in 1939, along with some civilian construction companies such as Siems Drake. They had "been in the process of changing the entire landscape" in Sitka for the military installations which were to follow. At that time, Sitka's population was maybe 2000 people or less. Fishing was the main source of employment, helped by the presence of an efficient Sitka Cold Storage, which provided aged ice and frozen herring, especially for the halibut fishermen who arrived from

Seattle and ports south. The longer ice is frozen, the denser it becomes and the more slowly it melts, so "aged ice" was in great demand by fishermen. Pyramid Packing was in full swing, canning the pink or humpback salmon. According to Roy, "Immediately after Pearl Harbor, people of Japanese descent were rounded up and marched down the street by military guard. Most of us thought that was quite peculiar as these people were friends and neighbors."

The Army and Navy were sending men by the hundreds to Sitka and surrounding islands, including Biorka Island, while the Coast Guard ruled the waterfront. After war was declared, Sheldon Jackson had to "black out" all its windows. Allen Auditorium had large, tall windows which had to be covered immediately. A "Home Guard" came into being and inspected windows nightly.

Construction changed Japonski Island from a pleasant wooded island into a fortress of military activity. The two large buildings now being used by Mt. Edgecumbe High School and the University of Alaska were actually airplane hangars where maintenance and repair work were carried out for the many PBY's, which were called "Catalina Flying Boats." They were amphibians with long wing spans, able to land on water or land. Their two engines were able to get them airborne, and fly for hours before they had to refuel. They covered a range far out into the North Pacific, doing search and patrol for foreign vessels. The charts for these flying boats are still on the walls of the "old control tower," which is now used as a storeroom. These charts contain the entire coast from Sitka to Kodiak, with large circles drawn for specifically assigned patrol areas.

I learned one amusing story which Roy remembers from that specific time, and which was also related to us by Sam Ferraro, a Pennsylvania man whom we befriended, and who was stationed along with his National Guard Unit from 1942 through 1944 on Biorka Island. One of the patrols sighted what was thought to be a submarine just off Cape Edgecumbe so they bombed said target and reported "sighted sub, sank same." The ocean turned a bright red. The sunken target was a humpback whale.

A draft board was activated and the local older boys found themselves instantly drafted. Many of them immediately volunteered for the Navy and were accepted. Most of these volunteers were already able-bodied seamen, and were almost immediately assigned to shipboard duty with little time at boot camp. The older girls found it delightful to see their classmates in uniform. Some of the younger boys became acquainted with a PBY pilot who regaled them with stories of long patrols out over the ocean. Roy briefly dabbled with the idea that being a pilot would be a great thing to do. As the only boy in his class, (all his male classmates, being older, had joined the military), he felt he had to "uphold the male rule to terrorize the girls." They promptly named him "The Little Monster." Being the only boy left in his class contributed to his decision to leave school at the end of his sophomore year in the spring of 1942 when he was only 15 years old. He had decided to spend a year with his dad until he too could join the Navy.

Somehow during this time, Roy's birth year was changed to 1925. We are not absolutely positive how this occurred because his Juneau Public School records clearly state that it was 1926. However, the BIA census in 1929 used his brother's birth date of 1923 for his. All of his military records show 1925. We suspect it happened during the summers in Sitka when he worked at Sitka Cold Storage. We think it may have been jogged up a year so that he could work alongside his classmates who were older than he. (The labor laws required that workers be 16.) In any event, the draft board had him registered with the birth date of 1925 and with no middle initial. So for years, his name on federal records listed him as Roy NMI Bailey, dob 11-5-25. Perhaps in order to compete with the boys in his new environment, he made himself a year older. No one required a birth certificate for proof of age back then, or perhaps the cannery did it in order to legally hire him before he was 16. In any event, when we finally secured an official birth certificate from the State of Alaska in 1978, it shows his name as Roy *Daniel* Bailey with 1926 as his year of birth. By that time, Charlie Sr. had died and we have no idea where the *Daniel* came from, but Roy has been thrilled to have a middle name, and loves to use it as part of his signature.

A terrible accident occurred during this time. Roy witnessed the accident and did the best he could to help. Charlie Daniels was walking down the ramp to ANB

Harbor late at night and fell to the rocks below, breaking a leg, and pushing the bone up through his groin, causing him excruciating pain. However, medical facilities, such as they were, were available only to the white population and were not available to Natives. Charlie was flown to Juneau where he eventually recovered. (As an aside of possible interest, Charlie owned the *F/V Empress* which Herman Kitka purchased and renamed the *F/V Martha K.*)

After quitting school, Roy went to work at the Cold Storage with his dad. He worked there until, according to his new birth date of 1925, he turned 17 in the fall of 1942. He bought his first car, a 1935 Plymouth. This purchase by itself labeled him as different than most of the Native boys, who for some reason, seldom considered buying a car. He remembers his father driving the car one day when he wasn't around, and his father being quite amazed by it. There were only a few autos in Sitka at that time.

As he had discovered from 3rd grade, Roy had problems living with his step-mother and even though he provided much of the meat for the table, he was still longing to join his classmates in the Navy. In late 1943, Charlie Sr. gave Roy enough money to get to Seattle. The recruiting office and the draft board had moved to Seattle by this time. He traveled by the Northland Transportation Company's vessel *The North Star*. He found the trip and scenery interesting, but landed in Seattle with very little money, so he went directly to the Navy Recruiting Office. When Roy got there, they asked him how much he knew about radar. He had never heard of radar. They told him they were only taking men who knew radar.

Roy was now in Seattle with no money and no useful information about what to do next. He decided he would try to phone his father in Sitka for help but he had never used a dial telephone before he got to Seattle. In his words, "Sitka didn't have any telephones available to the public. I guess my efforts to use a dial telephone [were] similar to a bear in a china closet with boxing gloves on. Finally an operator asked me what number I wanted. Now why didn't she do that earlier?"

A person would be in a lot of trouble leaving Alaska for the very first time and arriving in a big city if he didn't know how to read, according to Roy. After being refused by the Navy, he found the draft board office to sign up for the Army because he had no money and needed to do something. Now, his hope was to catch the *North Star* back to Sitka. After roaming the streets for a while, he ran into Al Perkins, a fellow Sitkan. He asked Al for a loan of $20 to tide him over. Al said no. Once a man signed up at the draft board, it took about three months before they called the man up. Al had just signed up, and was going back to Alaska on the *North Star* to wait until he was called up. Roy also ran into another man from Sitka, who also was not able to loan him $20 either.

Then he ran into Richard Paul from Wrangell who had been declared 4F (a term indicating that for health reasons, this person was not eligible for the military), and had just signed all the papers needed to classify him 4F. Richard was an SJ classmate of Roy's. Roy told Richard the predicament he was in. Richard said, "Well, come along with me. You can stay with me and I'll get you a job." So they went to the hotel where Richard was staying, and then to Northwest Steel Rolling Mills, where Roy went to work to earn enough money to keep himself sheltered and fed. Eventually, Roy was able to get his own room at the same place where Richard was staying so that he wouldn't be imposing. The steel mill melted down scrap metal by the ton for the war effort, and Roy worked with this molten metal. The work was physically difficult but Roy, with his unusual strength and staying power he had learned, didn't have any trouble with it. Roy claims it to be the hottest and dirtiest job he ever had, but "it was a job." He stayed there until the draft board called him into the Army.

He was drafted in the summer of 1944. He was sent to Camp Roberts in California (near Paso Robles – this military camp has since been closed) for basic training which, during WWII, lasted sixteen weeks. Here, he quickly learned that any Native from Alaska was automatically called an "Eskimo." It was pointless to try to educate those who had never heard about Tlingits or the way of life that existed in Southeast Alaska, as most people were sure they knew about the land of Alaska, a land which was "entirely ice and snow."

He made a small, close group of friends, the first he had ever had. Sharing the rigors of boot camp undoubtedly helped in the formation of this camaraderie. These men were all from Salt Lake City, Utah. Even with the heat and aridity of this area of California, Roy did well in boot camp, and was eventually chosen to become a paratrooper. This was an honor awarded to only a few of those being trained. However, when Roy found that he would have to forego leave given to those who finished their training and be separated from the friends he had made, he requested that his name be withdrawn.

Roy in boot camp

Upon "graduating" from boot camp, he took the train to Seattle, looked around for anyone he might know, and upon finding no one, he got on a train bound for Fort Benning, Georgia, where he was reunited with his Salt Lake City friends as they all waited to be deployed.

They shipped out in a large convoy, which was constantly on the lookout for German submarines even at this point in the war (early 1945). Most of the soldiers got seasick during the thirty-day crossing. Roy says he's never seen waves so big. They were told they were going through the end of a hurricane. Being sea-born, he enjoyed the trip across, and never missed a meal. He said he didn't know of anyone else who managed that.

They got to South Hampton, England, but were not allowed off the ship so they sat aboard, looking longingly at land. They went from there to Le Havre, France, where they disembarked with large mounds of supplies for the Army already there. They started their trek northward toward Berlin. He was in Company E, 5th Infantry Regiment of General Hodges' 7th Army, 71st Division, of heavy weaponry with 80mm mortars and machine guns. This was different than regular infantry, as the small squads manning a machine gun were frequently out ahead in "no man's land," keeping the regular infantry under cover of machine gun fire. They did not carry rifles, as they had their hands full taking care of the larger weapons. As the Army does not take friendships into consideration, at this point Roy and his friends were separated, and he never saw them again. He seldom talks about combat, as most soldiers who have seen combat do not talk about it.

By this time, the German Army may have been falling apart, (what was left of the German Army was sometimes young boys, old men, and women of all ages), but it was still a potent enemy. The Battle of the Bulge was continuing to the north and east. Roy came into this as one of the replacement troops for the huge number of troops lost in the Battle of the Bulge. As a private manning a machine gun or a mortar with four or five men to a squad, he had one of the most dangerous jobs there was.

Not all his traveling was by foot. Roy's unit spent four days traveling by troop train, "the Forty and Eight," so named because the cars held forty troops or eight horses. Then they would be back to hiking for miles until the heavy weapons squads would be told to take up a position somewhere "out there." Sometimes, they would get caught by small groups of German soldiers before they were positioned, and skirmishes took place in the dark of night.

On one occasion, Roy was sent with the other squad members to relieve a squad who had already taken up a position "out there". He was not carrying a rifle, only a part of a bazooka — a tank-destroying-type of large caliber gun. Roy says a better description of this would be a "rocket launcher" that is fired from the shoulder like a rifle is.

Unknown to him and his fellow soldiers, the U. S. had

sent out a "bang-up patrol" from Roy's squad's left-hand side. These bang-up patrols went out with large amounts of armaments and were charged with filling a certain location with everything in their arsenal to totally destroy everything within that specific location. At the same time, also unknown to both Roy's squad and the U.S. bang-up patrol, the Germans also sent out their own bang-up patrol from the right hand side of Roy's squad. They were traveling down a dirt road, which only had about a curb height indentation on the edge of the road. Roy's squad was in the middle, not knowing they were being converged upon by two bang-up patrols. They hit the dirt when all hell broke loose with grenades and shells suddenly coming at them from both sides. According to Roy, "The sound and light of the fury could only be described as *awesome* in all the superlatives that word can imply." Roy says, "[We] could tell which grenades were American because American grenades had a fuse that let off sparks." It was a miracle, that, even after the fireworks came at them from both sides, only one of his squad was hit.

After this event, all of Roy's squad made their way home on their own. How the others made their way he doesn't know because he couldn't move and he couldn't make a sound because the Germans were still all around. He was totally tangled in a gigantic web of wire that had been strung along the side of the road. The wire had caught in his ammunition belt, and immobilized him. It took him a lengthy time to get loose. While he was working on extricating himself, it grew quieter, and he could hear the German soldiers talking. A long period of time passed while he quietly listened to them talk. By the time he got loose, even the Germans had left the area. All he could think about was his knowledge that only one of his squad had been hit and that had been in the shoulder. The wounded squad member was able to leave the area on his own power. When Roy finally managed to make his way back to camp, he was challenged by a sentry who demanded a password. Roy's squad had not been given a password, because they had been on their way to relieve a machine gun squad; they had not been expected to return for several days, by which time a different password would be needed. Roy was angry, and told the sentry he didn't have a password and to let him pass or "he'd shoot their heads off." A second sentry told the first sentry, "Oh this is an American!" By this time, Roy had been reported as MIA, and that report was sent to his father. Unknown to Roy, this report was never corrected, and his father back home in Sitka was never notified that he was found. He went back to the same unit to which he had been assigned and it was another day and night - two nights altogether - before the squad was able to go back out and finally relieve the machine gun squad in no-man's land.

Another time when they were hiking ahead of the troops, they were fired upon from the belfry of a small church. They took shelter and tried to eliminate the sniper, whom they finally recognized as female. They were unable to do so. They had to call up a howitzer to blow the belfry off the church.

They were told not to drink the water without using tablets to purify the water, but that made the water so disagreeable to drink the men hated to use them. Sometimes they were able to go into French cellars instead, and drink the wine that most French people kept. The streams and water they passed during their travels were frequently filled with huge dead Belgian horses along with the other carnage of war. Roy says sometimes they were so thirsty that they simply drank the water with the blood in it — with or without purifying tablets. When they saw French citizens, they learned to ask for "oueffs" (eggs) which were rare, and incredible feasts were cooked up as quickly as possible when the eggs were given to them.

Another frequent occurrence Roy witnessed was the approach of unescorted enemy soldiers, with their hands on top of their heads, hoping to put an end to their war by surrendering. This would give them a release from impending death, and also would include a hand-out of American cigarettes and coffee. "If you took the time to look them in the face, you saw the face of a defeated, cold, hungry human being," according to Roy.

The job they had to do as soldiers was dirty and tiring, and was still very dangerous and volatile. Look at a map of Germany and France to picture the journey from Le Havre to Wiesbaden, which is just across the border into Germany from France about 50-60 miles. Roy got nearly as far as Wiesbaden where his squad was attacked. He was wounded by machine gun fire which badly damaged his right hand. He also received shrapnel wounds on his arm and other parts of his body. Of the four members of his squad, he was the only survivor.

He was evacuated to a Paris hospital where he heard the bells toll. Even today, he talks about how impressive these bells were to him. When there is talk of bells ringing, Roy always thinks of the bells in Paris.

Waiting for the evacuation from Paris to England, Roy realized that there was a very young German boy lying on a cot next to him in the hospital tent. The boy was so badly wounded that Roy doubts he survived. Everyone in the medical tent had been given coffee, and he noticed the boy was not drinking his. Being able to get up, and being Roy, he went over, picked up the cup, and offered to help the boy drink. The lad kept saying what sounded like "*Kalt,*" which Roy later learned means "cold" in German. The boy could not drink, as he was too cold. Roy weeps whenever this story is mentioned.

Later on, the word was out that there was an Eskimo wounded in the medical tent. Roy lifted himself up to sitting position, and was asked by a nurse what he thought he was doing. Roy said he was looking for the Eskimo. The nurse laughed, and told him that he was the Eskimo. Such was the life of a wounded Tlingit warrior in Paris.

He was in England a couple of months before he was sent to Walla Walla, Washington, for debriefing, psychological examination, and discharge. Post Traumatic Stress Syndrome was not in any vocabulary in WWII. Many who probably had this syndrome were belittled so most veterans seldom discussed what was happening to them. This was a devastating experience, as this is where he was challenged as to the truth of his description of his receipt of wounds. The psychiatrist indicated he did not believe that an "Eskimo" fighting in a squad with white men could have survived when the white men died. Therefore, the psychiatrist's conclusion was that his wounds had to have been accidental or self-inflicted. Roy was so traumatized by the treatment he received during the debriefing that until 1999, he refused to acknowledge any war service at any public event, and totally refused to talk about his experiences to anyone. He also says that the psychiatrist who interrogated him got him so rattled that he no longer knows anything about the event, other than it was neither accidental nor self-inflicted. He was just barely eighteen years old. The trauma of the questioning (and his combat experience) was real. As for me, I refuse to continue it.

An exacerbating event occurred while Roy was in Walla Walla. One evening, two of the soldiers there invited him to join them in an excursion into town. They went to a bar and ordered beers. Roy didn't drink at that time but enjoyed the camaraderie so he ordered one too. The bartender looked at him and said, "We don't serve Eskimos." This made the other men angry, so they shared their beer with Roy and ordered more. As Roy drank the beer, he became more upset about the situation, and decided to leave and go back to the hospital. He says that his thoughts were primarily focused on two things: not wanting to embarrass his fellow soldiers, and being denied a beer by the bartender because he was Eskimo. As he went back to the hospital, fueled by having drunk two or three beers, he got angrier and angrier, and when he got to the hospital, he had trouble opening the screen door so he simply tore it off its hinges and threw it aside. At his daily interview by the psychiatrist, he was asked, "Why are you so angry?"

When Roy was finally discharged, he received enough money to get him to Seattle but no further. Once again, he found himself alone and without the means to get to Sitka. Riding a city bus, he overheard two women who were talking about the end of the war. One of them indicated that if the war had lasted only six months more, she would have had enough money to purchase the curtains for her home that she had been wanting. Obviously, this comment was heard out of context, but such a comment hit a very resonant note in Roy's mind. It was beyond belief to Roy, who had suffered the complete journey to hell that defines war, that anyone could possibly want the war to last another six months. He telegraphed home, and his brother sent him enough money for passage on an Alaska Steamship Company vessel. When he got to Sitka, his step-mother Olinda, the first person he saw, said "What are you doing here? We thought you were dead."

In July of 2004, Roy went to a meeting of Native veterans

who live in Sitka. At that meeting, Mark Jacobs Jr. told a story that Roy had never heard nor known about. When Roy was listed as missing in action, his father Charlie became so upset that he went to the church and asked for prayer. What happened was that several of the churches in Sitka organized what would now be called a "prayer chain," and prayed for Roy and with Charlie every day until Roy arrived home. There was never any communication from the government about Roy "being found," so they didn't know until he returned home. Roy was extremely moved by this story, and wished he would have known so he could have thanked them in person, but many years have passed, and most of those involved are no longer with us. I should probably mention at this point that Roy never received any mail during WWII from anyone other than Dan Johnson from Angoon who sent him a letter. Dan Johnson was a classmate from Sheldon Jackson. Roy never forgot the letter received and has treasured the fact of his receiving it all his life.

A young Tlingit man named Robert Sam visited with Roy once in about 1996, and found out that Roy had never received any of the medals that he should have received from his service in WWII. Sometime later, Robert was in a position with Sitka Tribe to have personal contact with military people in the U. S. Department of Defense. Robert, along with Jack Lorrigan and Mark Jacobs, Jr., petitioned the Department of Defense for Roy to receive these medals. In 1998, Roy received a phone call from

Washington, D. C. asking about this. Roy hung up on them. He told me about the phone call, and I contacted Robert who gave me the name and phone number of the person who had called Roy. After I discussed the situation with Colonel Kurt Kratz, I asked Roy if he did not want to receive these medals. Roy's only comment was, "There is no way the U.S. Army is going to give me any medals. They will never change their minds." He was totally convinced that the U.S. Army firmly believed that no Indian could have fought in Europe, and been wounded in battle, and been the only survivor. He had no corroborating witnesses.

However, Mark Jacobs Jr. had laid the groundwork for Roy's cause as he served for many years as a member of the Department of Veterans Affairs Advisory Committee on Minority Veterans, and he had worked for ten years to get the recognition for Roy that he felt was appropriate. Robert Sam was unrelenting in his efforts to correct this sad chapter in Roy's life. When I got involved, there were a number of people in Washington, D.C. that had been convinced of the legitimacy of the request, and were working with the Secretary of the Army to do something about it. When I talked to Colonel Kurt Kratz, his main concern was that Roy would not want to receive the medals nor be recognized. I explained the dilemma to him, and we agreed that I needed to get Roy's permission and then they would proceed. Roy cautiously gave me his permission with two caveats:

1) He wanted his entire family there if it was to be a public recognition; 2) His permission was granted for one reason only — that this might help others who had been denied medals or recognition because of racial discrimination.

In the middle of these discussions with Colonel Kratz in the Department of Defense, Roy suffered symptoms of a heart condition, and we had to rush to Seattle for cardiac consultation. It was while we were in Seattle that Colonel Kratz and I were able to put the finishing touches on a presentation plan at the same time as Roy was being given a stent to open an artery in his heart. A hearing board was listening to Roy's case at that very time and the colonel called me when he had the medals in his hand.

On February 19, 1999, Roy Daniel Bailey was presented the Purple Heart, Combat Infantryman Medal, WWII Victory Medal, North African-European Theater Medal, and the Bronze Star by Secretary of Defense William Cohen and Alaska Senator Ted Stevens at Elmendorf Air Force Base, Anchorage, Alaska. Our three daughters, son and daughter-in-law, and five of our grandchildren, along with two representatives from Sitka Tribe, Robert Sam and John Nielsen, were present for the ceremony.

The one comment Roy made to me after the presentation was, "The medal that means the most to me is the Combat Infantryman Medal." The receipt of this medal does affirm, in fact, his combat duty.

*Representing Sitka Tribe of Alaska at the Award Ceremony
are John Nielson and Robert Sam*

THE ALASKA LEGISLATURE

HONORING

ROY BAILEY

The Twenty-first Alaska State Legislature joins friends and family in honoring Roy Bailey of Sitka, who has received the Purple Heart and Bronze Star for his service in the United States Army during World War II.

The Purple Heart is awarded in the name of the President of the United States to people who are wounded in the line of duty. The Bronze Star is awarded for heroism in battle against an enemy of the United States.

Roy Bailey was serving in Germany in 1945 in a unit fighting numerous battles in a push toward Berlin. Roy was wounded on the battlefield and was the only member of his unit to survive. After being taken to a hospital in England he returned to the United States and came home to Sitka. He was given an honorable discharge, but his papers did not reflect his heroism or battle wounds, prerequisites for receiving the medals. He lived fifty-four years without that honor.

Friends working with the Sitka Tribe of Alaska learned of Roy's experience and pursued a campaign with the Department of Defense to address a need to honor Native American veterans who were never given proper military recognition in war. Through their efforts and a commitment on the part of the Department of Defense, Roy Bailey's case was heard and he was finally given the awards he earned. In a ceremony in Anchorage on February 19, 1999, Secretary of Defense William Cohen and Senator Ted Stevens presented Roy with his medals.

The Alaska State Legislature is proud to honor Roy Bailey and offers its congratulations to him, his family, friends, and to members of the Sitka Tribe of Alaska for their dedication in this matter.

BRIAN PORTER
SPEAKER OF THE HOUSE

DRUE PEARCE
PRESIDENT OF THE SENATE

Date: March 3, 1999

BEN GRUSSENDORF
PRIME SPONSOR

Cosponsors: Representatives Porter, Austerman, Berkowitz, Brice, Cissna, Croft, Davies, Davis, Dyson, Harris, Hudson, James, Joule, Kemplen, Kerttula, Kohring, Kookesh, Morgan, Mulder, Murkowski, Phillips, Rokeberg, Smalley, Therriault, Williams; Senators Taylor, Lincoln, Hoffman, Pearce, Parnell, Tim Kelly, Pete Kelly, Elton, Mackie, Leman

*Secretary of Defense William Cohen presents Roy with his
medals for World War II in a ceremony at Elmendorf Air
Force Base, Anchorage, Alaska, on February 19, 1999.*

CHAPTER TEN

Basketball and More

Roy stayed at his father's house after he returned from the war only long enough for him to earn enough money to get his own place. His relationship with Olinda was still rocky and although he kept meat on the table, it seemed to him as though that was the only use he had. As Roy said to me, "I told Dad that as soon as I could earn enough money, I would be getting my own place. Dad understood." Being a vet recently returned from war, he didn't have any trouble getting work. Among the things he did after returning from war was work for Columbia Lumber Company, driving a lumber carrier, and he worked for the City of Sitka driving a truck. (He got scolded once for driving through a big puddle of water and splashing a person walking on the side of the road.)

Roy also was involved with the Alaska Native Brotherhood.

He remembers going to a Grand Camp convention in Angoon right after World War II. Travel to convention or to basketball games was always by fishing vessels, usually seiners. Peter Simpson is the revered and much honored founder of the Alaska Native Brotherhood. He was educated at the Presbyterian industrial school at Sheldon Jackson. Peter Simpson, by this time very old and infirm, was helped up the ladder at the dock by the young and strong men such as Roy. (Isabella Brady is his granddaughter.)

Anyone living in Southeast Alaska either played or watched basketball. It was THE favorite activity enjoyed by the entire population. When the military had "invaded" Sitka in 1938, it was not long before basketball tournaments were being held between numerous teams made up of military, their attendant civilian contracting crews, and the population of Sitka. Roy says, "Of our teams, there were the 'bar' teams and, of course, our ANB (Alaska Native Brotherhood) team. Of the military and others, it amazed me when they said most of their team members were in college at one time or another. Awesome playing against college men in those days! Gradually, we became the team to beat. Our team bought their own uniforms with ANB colors and lettering. That gave us added incentive to play a bit more meaningful to beat those college guys. Quite often, we did beat them and quite handily. Our players were Nick Kasakan as center, as he was the tallest guy, Moses Johnson and Jimmy Walton [as] the forwards and Joe Truitt and I were the guards. Joe was the running guard and I was the standing guard, which was mainly in the back court as the action went on. Back then, basketball was a "no contact sport." As a standing guard, I was relegated to the back court unless the action got fast and furious. Then I joined in the fray of the fast moving game. Being of small stature as compared to our opponents made us rather fast dribblers and down low. But getting the ball to Moses or Jimmy or Nick was the goal as they were the best shooters! We honed that to almost perfection. Our home town fans were our cheerleaders and spurred us on even more. Moses Johnson's expertise soon became known up and down the west coast, and other towns began getting teams together to beat that ANB team from Sitka."

In the prelude to becoming the host of the well-known "Gold Medal Tournament," Juneau started inviting teams there to play a round robin schedule. According to Roy, "The first time out we got beat by Ketchikan so [we] had to go the basement route to try to get back into the play-offs. One of the games we had to play was against Douglas High School. You can imagine the cheering for Douglas as they were now pitted against one of the power house teams, the Sitka ANB. Believe it or not, but we had a devil of a time beating those high school kids. Matter of fact, we looked kind of silly, as how much pressure do you put on [defeating] high school kids? It was a memorable game and we congratulated the high school team for being good and dedicated players. We won the tournament that year, even after having gone the basement route. Our mode of transportation to and from Juneau was via seine boat. We also paid our own hotel bill. On the way home, we stopped in Angoon. Angoon promptly put together their team and challenged the ANB team from Sitka. Angoon won! I played basketball for a few years going to Juneau for their invitational tournament each year.

"Later, we went over on the *Mt. Edgecumbe*, a combo passenger and freight boat for Mt. Edgecumbe School. On one trip coming back to Sitka, we hoisted a broom high on the mast to indicate a "clean sweep" at the tournament. But by now, the imported players began to make a showing. It was fun in those days. What amused me was how old some of those military guys were – some were bald or nearly so. Anyway, it was fun and I moved off the team and other young fellas came in. Change was in the air and I went my own way."

After the job with the City, Roy got a job for the BIA (Bureau of Indian Affairs), operating a shore boat (the *Teddy*), and driving a bus on Japonski Island. Roy was one of three men that were hired to patrol the island for security. This was where Roy met Fred Geeslin, who proved to be a difficult but usually fair administrator of Japonski Island. The tuberculosis sanatorium had opened for Natives from all over the State of Alaska, and most of the people Roy transported had tuberculosis. In those days, no thought of protecting employees existed. No one understood exactly how tuberculosis was transmitted. The job included living quarters and meals on the island. Roy was able, with relief, to move into the single men's quarters on Alice Island.

When the military left Sitka after World War II, they simply abandoned all the buildings and some of the equipment. Then some of the buildings were used together as a hospital, first as a crippled children's hospital, and then as a tuberculosis sanatorium. The TB epidemic grew so large that a hospital was built just for that purpose. Nurses were greatly in demand, hired directly out of nursing school and were called "cadet nurses." Dorothy Thomsen, called "Brownie," Marge Ward, Marlys Tedin, and Mary Ann Perkins (Al's wife) were among several who still live here in Sitka who arrived early as nurses for the TB hospital. The protocol for treating tubercular patients was, in Roy's words, "gruesome." Various surgeries were performed such as removal of ribs, crushing of the phrenic nerve to immobilize a lung, etc. His description reminded me of the experimental treatments performed on people with polio during that epidemic in the 1950's. Not knowing what caused these diseases, doctors were free to try to help patients in whatever manner they deemed appropriate. Roy has always felt the experimentation happened because the patients were "Indian" and, therefore, more radical theories could be explored with professional "immunity."

During these years, activity on Japonski, Alice, and Charcoal Islands was intense. The housing for the single "cadet nurses" became known as "Heifer Inn," a sexist and politically incorrect term for the 21st century. The single males were housed in a building soon known as "Empty

Arms Hotel."

The two airlines active in the State of Alaska at this time were Pan American and Trans World Airlines. A Pan American flight on its way north to Anchorage developed mechanical problems near Sitka and had to ditch in the ocean. The FAA supply boat for Biorka Island was handy and ready to help. The skipper was Ed Littlefield, a Native friend whose brother had been a close buddy of Roy's, and he rescued all the passengers from the downed plane. Later, the Coast Guard came along and demanded that all the passengers be transferred to their ship since it was bigger. Only in the transfer was there any injury. Once again, Ed's being "Indian" seemed to cause the media reports to refer only to the Coast Guard as having "saved" the passengers.

Roy met and married Eva Clark, twenty years his senior, who was working on Alice Island as a cook. They moved into married quarters in Millerville. Roy and Eva had only been married a short time when Roy was diagnosed with tuberculosis.

He was in a dangerous predicament because the BIA had a policy whereby employees could not be treated at the BIA hospital. Finally, the VA said they would be responsible for his treatment, and he was allowed in the TB sanitarium on Japonski Island.

He was there for nine months flat on his back. During this time, he painted pictures. His favorite subjects were the wild animals with which he was familiar, and boats. He used his own hair tied to a stick for a brush; the hospital had a few watercolors available for patient's use as there was no money to buy anything frivolous. He also carved the small totem pole that we have displayed in our home. His pictures are beautiful. He definitely had and has an artist's heart.

One of Roy's drawings

About that time, streptomycin with PAS (para amino salicylate) came into being. It was the only medication that cured TB. This was in 1950, when antibiotics were just beginning to be heard of and used. The IHS (Indian Health Service) did not have enough money to give their Native patients this new "wonder" drug, but Roy was being taken care of by the VA, and received the new medication, which soon allowed him to be discharged.

Nobody believed yet that a person could survive TB, so he was told to go home, but not to do anything. Essentially, it was felt he would probably be an invalid the rest of his life. He simply ignored this prognosis, and went about fixing the house he and Eva had just bought, replacing the roof, and refinishing the beautiful hardwood floors inside.

On Japonski Island, there were two large housing developments where married people working on the island lived. One was Igaroti Village where the FAA (Federal Aviation Administration) employees and families lived, and the other was the larger Millerville.

Most of those living in Millerville worked for Public Health, later BIA (now SEARHC - Southeast Alaska Regional Health Consortium, a Native-owned facility). From the many governmental and intertwined uses of the island, it is easy to understand why the "ownerships" of parcels on Japonski have been difficult to sort out and boundaries set. Currently, those boundaries have finally been resolved and clarified with the cooperation of the State of Alaska, (Mt. Edgecumbe High School, airport and University of Alaska), Shee Atika Corporation, City and Borough of Sitka, SEARHC, and the U.S. Coast Guard. The small parcel where the old boat house is located has been transferred to the City and Borough so that it can be turned into an historical maritime museum managed and leased by the non-profit Sitka Maritime Heritage Society.

In June of 2004, Roy and I went into the woods where

Millerville existed and found the house where Roy and Eva had lived. Roy was quite amazed at finding it. The alders have grown over the whole area, and most of the buildings were succumbing to the rainforest. It reminded us of how Biorka Island has been overgrown with alders. Alders grow anywhere the land has been disturbed, and the whole of Japonski was "disturbed" during military occupation.

The house in Millerville used to have a fabulous view out over the ocean and islands before, of course, the expansion of the airport, building of the O'Connell Bridge, and the large amount of fill that has been added. The houses were primarily duplexes. The other couple that lived in the same house was Laura Jones and her husband, who had spent several years in the far north. She wrote Hearth in the Snow, a book which I found for Roy in a used book search a few years ago. She later became a professor at the University of Alaska. As Roy said to me, "Those were good years."

The houses in Millerville were abandoned because they contained asbestos, we have been told, but have recently been demolished and the area is being cleaned up by SEARHC. Sometimes Japonski Island is referred to as "Mt. Edgecumbe" by long time residents of Sitka. There was a U.S. Post Office on Japonski which used the name "Mt. Edgecumbe" as the address. That post office was closed in 1984. Old-time residents still refer to Japonski as Mt. Edgecumbe. Others simply refer to it as "the Island," and usually that includes both Alice and Charcoal Islands, which have been joined to Japonski in the building of the bridge and other activities using fill.

The other housing area on Japonski Island was Igaroti Village, where the FAA families lived. All these families (from both Igaroti Village and Millerville) got their groceries from Sitka. They could take the shore boat over, or they could phone their orders in and the grocery stores would deliver them to the shore boat, very much as we did when we lived on Biorka Island in the 70's.

After Roy and Eva were married, Roy started thinking about getting more education so that he would be eligible to secure a more-skilled job. He thought perhaps a trade such as heavy equipment operator might be something he would like to do. According to Roy, "Even that field was pretty much closed to Indians. The VA gave me a high school equivalency exam that I passed with no problem and so I decided to try for electronics school." In Sitka, a white man who shall remain unnamed approached Roy when he heard that Roy was planning to go to radio school to make the comment "That's a bit much for you to be trying to do, isn't it?"

The VA sent Roy to Oregon Technical Institute in Klamath Falls, Oregon, a trade school for radio repair. Roy comments, "Boy, what a challenge that was. I immediately ran into higher math that was the crux of all the learning. But not being a quitter I kept my head down, studied hard, morning, day, and night, and got through school."

The GI bill helped pay the bills, and Eva worked, and they made it through the two-year course in three years. During the summers, he worked for Tule Lake Lava Beds National Park. After he completed Oregon Tech, Roy went to work for United Airlines in San Francisco. He worked there until the recession of 1957 and he was laid off. He went back to Klamath Falls, where he went to work for Weyerhaeuser Timber, taking care of their communications and electrical equipment. They wanted him to continue, but he got a job with Baraboo Electric working on radios and televisions. He and the owner of that company became good friends, and he stayed until he went to work in 1960 for the Civil Aeronautics Agency, which became the Federal Aviation Administration.

In the meantime, while he was at Oregon Tech, he met a young man from Homedale, Idaho, whose name was Warren Nanney. Warren was also attending Oregon Tech "radio school." The two became friends. Warren was not married at that time. They were reunited when they met in 1963 in San Jose, California, both of them working for the Federal Aviation Administration. By this time, Roy and Eva had separated and divorced. Warren's wife became a widow, and soon after that she and Roy were married. And the rest, as they say, is history!

Roy's life has been *"A Divided Forest."* He belongs to an entire generation who each in his or her own way, and with varying degrees of success, has had to learn, individually, how to navigate the divided forest. Now in his 80's, it has been a significant and important exercise for Roy to connect the dots to his cultural identity.

Even though separated from a traditional Tlingit upbringing, he is a model of traditional Tlingit values such as respect, humility, helping others, and honoring the past and his culture. He has become a role model, an avid dispenser of encouragement, a bridge between cultures, and a quiet but insistent supporter of those younger than he. He is becoming more comfortable in traditional settings, relentlessly pursuing his cultural heritage, and frequently is a silent but determined presence. He has used legendary Tlingit strength to get through his trials and to forge a positive spirit. He is a true *Tlingit warrior (X̱'eigaa K̲aa)* in the best sense of the word, both in Tlingit and in English.

Roy and Doris Wedding picture December 14, 1973.

Roy is flanked by his niece Jennifer Young (Mary Duncan's daughter) and Jennifer's son, Mitchell Young, as Roy is dressed in the treasured Chilkat blanket and Beaver hat of Deishú hít of the Deisheetaan at the koo.éex' for Mark Jacobs, Jr. on September 2, 2007. The description of the blanket and hat appear on the back cover of this book. Photo courtesy of David Dapcevich SitkaPhotos.

Additional readings suggested:

The Day We Paid for a Crime We Didn't Commit by Harold Jacobs

Matilda Kinnon Paul Tamaree, Tlingit Missionary in Southeast Alaska by Bonnie J. Gerow.

Haa Aaní, Our Land: Tlingit and Haida land rights and use, Goldschmidt, Walter Rochs, Sealaska Heritage Foundation 1998

Haa Kusteeyí, Our Culture, Tlingit Life Stories. By Dauenhauer, N. & R. Seattle: University of Washington Press

Early Views: Historical Vignettes of Sitka National Historical Park by Kristen Griffin

Link to Tlingit language curriculum for school districts from Sealaska Heritage Foundation:

http://www.sealaskaheritage.org/programs/language_and_culture_curriculum.htm

Authentic Indians by Paige Raibmon, Duke University Press Durham and London 2005

Will The Time Ever Come? A Tlingit Source Book edited by Andrew Hope III and Thomas F. Thornton

ISBN 142513761-X